I wanted only two things: a blatant display of her body to drive me wild with lust, and her own sheer natural indecency to make her lose all sense of inhibition and shame . . .

LILIANE

Paul Verguin

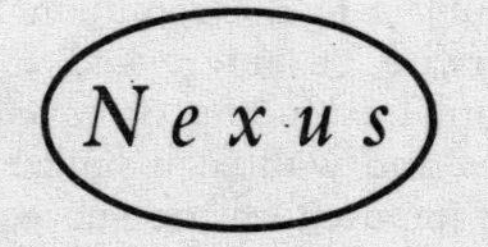

A Nexus Book
Published in 1991
by the Paperback Division of
W H Allen & Co plc
338 Ladbroke Grove
London W10 5AH

Phototypeset by Input Typesetting Ltd, London
Printed and bound in Great Britain by
Cox & Wyman, Reading, Berks.

ISBN 0 352 32785 5

Liliane

1

She was contrary. Peverse, that's the only way to describe it. She was determined to keep me guessing, to keep everything formal, right up to the last minute.

I'd met her for the first time only about two hours earlier at a dinner party with some friends in my apartment block. She'd struck me as intelligent – that is, if intelligence can be defined as the ability to skirt round subjects that people feel strongly about.

Her first name? Liliane. Her age? Not old, not even mature, but not young either. A chic Parisienne, about thirty years old, was my guess. Her profession? A radio journalist.

No doubt any man would have found her exciting. I certainly did. She wasn't wearing a bra, for one thing. During the meal I felt I wasn't sitting next to a person so much as a pair of soft, tantalising breasts. Yet apart from that constant distraction she could have been any woman whom I happened to meet at the home of some mutual friends.

She was wearing a one-piece outfit with long

puffed sleeves that displayed her long shapely legs. The material was silky, almost flesh-coloured, with blue and red embroidered stitching all over it. The neckline was held open by little metal rings sewn into the material. On her feet she wore red dancing shoes.

She had a mass of dark brown hair cut quite short. There was a hint of blue on her eyelids. Her lips and fingernails were the same bold shade of tomato red as the tiny stitches in her suit.

Over dinner we discussed furniture and interior design, and later on she asked me if she could see my flat. For all the notice she took of them, my friends might not even have been there.

In the lift, alone together, I felt we were shooting upwards to make love. But, as is usual with me, I didn't do anything about it, though I was absolutely certain that what she wanted was sex. I remember being almost shocked by the knowledge. Yet I dithered and prevaricated and failed to move in on her, keeping my awareness and sexual tension to myself.

She wasn't even my type. I didn't like her nose, it was too severe. I didn't like the way she talked, demanding all the attention for herself. At least, that's how it seemed to me at the time.

There was really quite a lot I didn't like about her. But then, I suppose I'm a bit perverse too, because I really fancied her. There were little lines at the corners of her eyes. For some reason they triggered off in me a fantasy that she was sex-mad, desperate for it, unable to say no.

I had all this running through my mind yet I said nothing to her whilst we were alone, enclosed in the lift together rushing upwards. There I was, on my way to my flat with a desirable willing woman, but I told myself I shouldn't trust to my own luck. I chattered politely, sticking to safe subjects but at the same time trying to convey that what was really on my mind was what was happening between the two of us, what we were about to do.

When we reached my floor I quickly led the way to my door and opened it for her. When I had first moved in to the apartment I had had a useless partition removed so that we were in the main room as soon as we stepped over the threshold.

'Oh, that's fantastic! What a terrific idea. I love it. Where do you get your ideas from?'

You know your own place like the back of your hand, so there are no distractions. I concentrated on watching her, as entranced with her as she seemed to be with my place.

Her one-piece garment was made out of that thin material – very fashionable at the moment – that emphasises the very contours of the body it pretends to cover. It's outrageously revealing. I couldn't decide which bits to concentrate on watching. I'd been sitting next to her all through dinner, and then I'd stood next to her in the intimacy of the lift, but I couldn't remember how big her breasts were. They certainly weren't small, but were they really large, or only average? I needed to check. But she crossed her arms over them then, as if exposure of her tits at that moment would compromise her and reveal the depths of her sexual obsession.

While we went round the apartment I tried to feast my eyes on her rear, but I was to be continually frustrated. I kept getting into positions from which I could hardly see a thing. I think we were both reluctant to take the plunge and I certainly had a sort of stage-fright but we were also getting impatient with our own awkwardness.

Liliane pretended to take a close interest in a dilapidated office chair that I had rather cleverly converted into an occasional table for indoor plants. I could tell she knew I was standing behind her, lusting after her. I think she was loving it, yet she seemed half-paralysed. I tried all the tricks I could think of to get her to lean forward to expose the curves of her arse, but nothing worked. We had become so hypersensitive that we were aware of each other's breathing. (Most of the time we just keep breathing without noticing that we are doing it; it is as if we can't pay any attention to these little things unless we are consumed by desire.)

I could see she had a slim waist although the tops of her hips were just a little too broad to put her in the top class of pretty little female arses. I didn't care. I wanted only two things:

a blatant display of her body to drive me wild with lust, and her own sheer natural indecency to make her lose all sense of inhibition and shame.

I tried very hard to make sure I smiled every time she glanced in my direction. I could tell I was smiling crookedly: I could feel my lips quivering at the corners. She must have been able to see through me; I'm sure she could read everything going through my mind. *We'll do whatever turns you on*, I was shouting inwardly, *and anything you don't like, I don't like either. If you are into anything unusual – flagellation, being whipped, anything – then that's just what I'm into, too . . .*

I wanted Liliane so badly that I would have agreed to anything she wanted. She must have been able to understand the look of hungry yearning that was plastered on my face. I did my best to keep my voice steady.

'I'll let you find your own way to the bathroom, then, if you need it. I'll just go and fix some drinks.'

She gave me a look that said she knew just what was going on. I withdrew to the kitchen where I had to sit down immediately. My legs were quivering even more than my fixed smile.

My prick was aroused, so much was obvious, but it felt strange. It seemed almost unreal. Like my knees, it felt stuffed with cotton wool, but the cotton wool was red hot. Did I have an erection? That was the question. I had to touch it to be sure. Of course I did. It was enormous, but it felt distant, as though it wasn't part of my body. Suddenly, I gained an insight into what it might be like to handle another man's erect penis. There I was, sitting in my own kitchen fondling a massive erection bulging out the material of my trousers – it was undeniably mine, yet it felt completely and curiously new to me.

For a moment I had a remarkable vision of what it would be like to desire myself, to be the narcissistic object of my own passion. I decided there and then that life in love with myself would be a beautiful and poetic adventure, though a little depraved, perhaps, sexually speaking.

I put it all down to Liliane: her equivocal attitude to getting down to sex had put me indirect touch with my own libido – I'd ended up playing with myself.

I could guess that the same thoughts were going through her mind for I heard splashing noises coming from the bathroom. At once I was in a reverie about soft, warm, pinknesses; freshly-showered clinging wet rosy places offered to me unendingly.

I came to, realising I was daydreaming. I stretched my arms, aflame. I stood up straight and the very fact of being alive gave me an electric shock of physical pleasure.

Standing in front of the sink I opened my flies and took out my prick. It was magnificent. It was stiff as an iron bar. I turned on the tap, and the jet of cold water was a cataract falling onto a smooth sun-warmed rock. I took out a clean tea-towel, folded it, and hung it over my stiffness as if over a heated towel-rail.

Once I had taken hold of my prick I couldn't let it go. The cloth had already soaked up the moisture but I continued reverently to move it backwards and forwards along my prick as though taking part in some sacred rite, rather than mundanely finishing off washing my penis. Still stroking myself, I turned off the tap with my left hand.

There was no sound in the apartment. Silence, I reflected, is a blanket under which we perform certain hidden acts, of which the most important is collusion.

When I came to my senses I released my grip on my prick and stuffed it back inside my trousers. With uncharacteristic skill and speed I threw ice and slices of lemon into two tall glasses and topped them up with gin and mineral water. As I left the kitchen I couldn't help noticing that my most valuable possession was still taking up most of the room between my stomach and my waistband.

I found Liliane gazing admiringly at a marvellous lithograph by my friend Jean-Claude.

I handed her one of the glasses. She downed the drink in one as if it had been just water. I did the same; I could tell by this time that we would both have to get a bit tipsy before we dared to admit that we both wanted to take advantage of the situation. I think that neither of us, sober, could really believe this was happening.

'This is ridiculous,' she said. 'All these details!'

Jean-Claude has a mania for cluttering up his compositions with tiny houses and the people inside them. No matter how long you stare at one of his pictures you can never be sure that you've found everything that's going on.

Then, quite suddenly, our debauch started.

She was standing in the space behind the studio couch. By subtle use of body-language, she made it obvious that she was going to stay exactly where she was, pretending to examine every inch of the lithograph. She remained leaning forward, her neck stretched up, holding her empty glass in her left hand just in front of her right breast. She had started to lose her inhibitions: inch by inch she was pushing her arse backwards in my direction.

I had to make a difficult decision. Should I stand immediately behind her, so that my protuberant crotch would nestle between her advancing buttocks, or, alternatively, should I move slightly to one side, so that the front of my trousers would come into contact with her right hand which was resting on her hip with the thumb hooked into a pocket? In the time I took to wedge my glass between the cushions at the back of the couch, I had made up my mind. I took a step to the right.

I, too, pretended to study Jean-Claude's panorama of village life, drawing Liliane's attention to some of my favourite characters. Under cover of this innocent chatter I started to move slowly forward, leading with my pelvis. Standing so near to her I was pretty sure that she was already aroused. As the distance between our bodies decreased I actually started to feel her warmth. She was burning, radiating heat like the sun itself. Now I was on fire; the whole of my left side, right up to my face, was glowing with her heat.

Conscientiously I pointed out each tiny house and its minuscule inhabitants, the even tinier children and animals, the exquisite detail of the trees and the railings alongside the narrow pavements. Here and there across the picture there were wittily erotic tableaux, but I didn't want to draw her attention to these yet. I was beginning to think that I wasn't getting anywhere by edging forwards: there still seemed to be a gulf between our bodies as wide as that which separates a rabbit-punch from a gentle kiss on the nape of the neck. Yet Liliane didn't move away. I began to suspect she was teasing me, making me wait. Then it occurred to me she was doing this for her own benefit, so that she could savour infinitely the delayed moment of contact. Would she be prepared to take the initiative? My heart beat rapidly as I forced myself to stand quite still, waiting for her to make the move that would bridge the gap between our bodies.

I didn't have to wait long. She made it look

so simple. Her first touch was light as a feather, but unmistakeable. The warmth of the palm of her hand seeped through the wool and cotton of my clothing and mingled with the heat of my erection. I leant a little towards her. A moment later, without her moving her hand from its position on her hip against my crotch, Liliane did the same, leaning closer to me.

I swear I heard a buzzing in my ears. My legs trembled so much I thought I'd collapse. I decided the time had come to point to the open window of one of the miniature houses through which a tiny couple could be seen enthusiastically fucking. The woman was sitting astride her partner who was gripping her waist with both hands. The woman's arms, stretched triumphantly above her head, thrust her breasts forward into the man's face. Keeping my groin pressed against Liliane, I let my left hand drop to my side and started moving my hip towards her curved bottom.

'Look,' I blurted hoarsely. 'Can you see? There – through the window, in that little house.'

'No – where? What is it?' Liliane was finding it as difficult to speak as I was.

She leaned forward a little more. I gave up staring at the lithograph and dropped my gaze to her hand on the front of my trousers. She caught the movement of my eyes and, as if she had been waiting for me to look at what she was doing, she started to stroke her hand up and down.

Dizzily my head swung down. The fine fabric of her dress clung to her so closely it was like a second skin. I could see the line of her knickers – I imagined them to have the texture of a chiffon scarf. Otherwise she looked naked, as if her warm fawn skin was bare save for its ornamentation of intricately-worked red and blue tattooing. And despite those knickers, the two cheeks of her arse were clearly defined, as rounded and as separate as the most voluptuous of female bottoms that have filled my fantasies since adolescence, a state I have never quite abandoned.

I was still content to look, but Liliane tempted me to touch. She placed her left hand, still holding the glass, on the wall beside the picture, and she took some of her weight on her left arm. Then she was able to part her legs a little more, curving her spine, pushing her bottom further back and up. She was determined to exhibit every curve and hollow of her buttocks as she slowly moved them inexorably towards my waiting hand. But her eyes never left the miniaturised antics of the couple in the picture, even as the cheeks of her arse inched towards the moment of contact.

Liliane's buttocks, as I have mentioned, were a little on the large side. They were beautifully curvaceous, but looked heavy and muscular. Therefore I was surprised when my fingers encountered soft and yielding flesh. I suspected that her buttocks were going to be as passionately tender as her breasts had promised to be at dinner. And if they were really as soft and tactile as her tits, then from my point of view they would actually be even better. I've always found bottoms more exciting than breasts, although it has to be said, that what with all the sexual tension and the hefty slug of gin, almost anything at that moment would have felt soft to me.

Without another moment's hesitation, I inserted my knuckles into the enticing hollow between her arse-cheeks. She must have been waiting for me to do it, because she immediately started moving, sliding her arse back and forth against my fingers.

'Oh!' she murmured in a very low voice, 'But that's ever so rude . . .' She made out she was talking about the lascivious couple in the picture. I suppose she was hoping that our mutual pleasure, exquisite but unspoken, would continue indefinitely. Or perhaps, while unable quite to resist surrendering to her own sensual urges, she was reminding us both that we couldn't carry on groping each other's private parts for ever as if somehow our bodies were in contact by accident.

At last she stopped staring at the picture. She lowered her head and turned it to the right to look at me. At first she looked down, as if her eyes were too heavy to lift, and she watched her hand as it stroked the shape of my erection through my clothes. Her hand was in an awkward position, upside down and caressing me from the front, but she had unhooked her thumb from her pocket and even through two layers of material I could feel her long fingers squeezing me. She was actually gripping me surprisingly tightly, considering that this was our first meeting.

I think she was trying to smile as she watched the movements of her hand, but I could see her face succumbing to an irresistible expression of abandoned lust – it would have been called lasciviousness in the days when such feelings were considered sinful. She was getting excited by watching what she was doing to me, and the fact that she was letting me see her state of excitement only added to her enjoyment. I could see that she was becoming confident with me. She already knew enough about me to know I would have no qualms about fuelling my own arousal by watching her lose control.

She raised her eyes by degrees to my waist, to my chest, and to my mouth. Her eyes sought mine. As our eyes met, she suddenly became the physical embodiment of an erotic fantasy. It wasn't just the way she was standing, her bottom thrust out towards me and her hand hot and tight on my prick; it was also the voiceless look of desire in her face, as if she was thinking *yes! yes! yes!* She was a dream – one of those febrile, impossible couplings that we yearn for when we are hungry for sex. She was a dream come true.

With her whole body she announced: *I'll do anything you want!* She didn't need to use words. She was like the star of some silent blue film, glowing with soundless sensuality.

I remembered with surprise that an hour earlier, when she had been chattering away on conventional topics of conversation, I had hardly found her attractive at all.

I uncurled my hand so that I could stroke her arse with my palm and my fingertips. I pushed, I caressed, I kneaded. I explored the entire surface. I loved every square inch of it.

She started to breath heavily. She wasn't quite moaning, but strange noises were coming from her throat. I was beginning to feel rather disorientated. My passions were at fever pitch and I had a sincere desire to give her a good time, but, though this is incredible, I wasn't quite sure I was up to the job. Even the most experienced and caring lover, awash with feelings of intense gratitude and very anxious to gain his pleasure in consideration of his partner's, can forget sometimes that sex requires a little selfishness now and again so that both can derive the maximum of pleasure.

Liliane continued to make slight movements, opening herself more and more to my groping hand. Occasionally she would flinch away, but only to increase the delightful suspense of gradually lifting her arse towards my waiting hand once more. I found this spectacle so attractive that sometimes I found myself unable to move my hands in response. Then she would rub her buttocks against my hand as if determined to break my apparent self-control.

She was till giving me that sidelong look. She seemed to be waiting for me to lift my eyes from her arse to meet her gaze. That would be her signal to take her turn at manual stimulation. With her fingers still pointing to the floor and her palm resting flat against my groin, she started to rub me as vigorously as she could. She managed to do this without hurting me. I could sense that, like myself, she had no interest in inflicting anything but pure pleasure, and that was all she wanted.

So I discovered how a woman's hands and her fingers can be the lewdest and most exciting of erogenous zones, at the limits of indecency. My cock and Liliane's hand made love together. I trembled helplessly in the grip of her astonishing caresses, surrendering myself utterly to her and abandoning myself to helpless overmastering lust.

I was making a great deal of noise. We both were. Sometimes I tried to keep my eyes closed so as to experience the pleasure more intensely but then I had to open them again to convince myself of the reality of what was taking place. Her eyes, when they met mine, said always the same thing – *yes! yes! yes!* – letting me sink into a sexual abyss.

I didn't know how long this could last. Liliane was stretched out delightfully before me always pointing that arse of hers up at me. Soon we would move on to more total activity, plunging into the sordid joyous depths without let or hindrance.

Yet I wanted this to go on for ever. How could I want it to stop? We just stood there, fully dressed, playing with one another. I fondled her sublime arse and she stroked my raging cock and though we both longed to feast at Love's groaning table, yet we contented ourselves meanwhile with titbits, titillating ourselves with morsels before the glut to come. I touched everything, every hollow, every swelling, her intoxicating valley. I fed on Liliane.

We shared our hunger, and we shared an ability to wait, to abstain from the climax that eventually each would help each to attain. We had to stroke, to caress, to fondle continuously and we had to be stroked, be caressed and be fondled at the same time. And all in the right places at the right time. On pain of death I could not have said what I preferred, whether to stroke the arse of Liliane through her clinging costume or whether to submit my cock, still protected by my trousers, to the firm strong caresses of her sexy hand. What did she prefer? I tried to make sure that it was what I was doing to her arse. I paid infinite attention to her. I was firm and yet I was gentle. In all, I think I was pretty good at it. At the same time I found the material of her clothes unspeakably sexy, and beneath it her panties tantalised and aroused me further. I surely had a natural talent for doing to my lovers that which gave supreme enjoyment to myself.

I could sense what she wanted, sense with my eyes and my fingers and my cock. I could sense that never before had she been so overwhelmed by desire. We can never know what our partners are like when they fuck other people but I guessed that with Liliane a certain prudishness usually remained, a sense of shame that might be some old hangover of the idea of sin taught in our youth. Now, with me as her lover, this was gone. As for myself, I felt that for the first time I had lost my fear of naivety and sexual clumsiness.

Perhaps we just met at the right time, when we both ready to slough off inhibition and fuck freely for the first time without complications crowding out the essential magic of the act.

We were still standing locked together beside my studio couch where the floor was parquet tiles. Our heavy breathing was eloquent and tumultuous, yet I heard her feet move. She wore those red dancing shoes. I had trainers on. Then I realised what she was trying to do. She was altering the way she stood to better expose her crotch. She was fabulously lewd!

I was genuinely touched by her consideration for me, almost sobbing with joy, and when she caught the sounds of my excitement and distress she opened her legs still further, more perhaps even than she had intended to. She let go of my groin and put down her glass. She pressed both hands against the wall, moved her feet back a little and splayed her cheeks properly open before me. I stepped back to give her room. I stepped back again to get a good look. I was almost behind the studio couch now. She was moaning in a low rough desperate voice, her shoulders heaving in excitement and I wondered how long she had contained this fantasy she now gave way to, of exposing herself, damp with sexual heat, to a man.

I couldn't keep away from her. Supercharged with frustrated desire I took hold of her again and began to touch what I longed for. My hand began to explore underneath and beyond, moving up to the stomach where her flesh was softly rounded. I remembered those naked breasts and my hand went on and up till I found their firmness. They hung down and as I touched the nipples they swung delightfully, heavy and totally satisfying. I felt like crowing like a cockerel at the way things were going, getting better all the time. I nearly made a complete fool of myself then as if I was an inexperienced buffoon, wanting to spout fine words when what was wanted was for me to grin and get on with the job in hand.

I longed for her breasts but I was prepared to wait for them, to wait for the right moment. I drew my arm back through her thighs with my fingers wide apart so that I could caress her stomach with my nails. I cupped my hand, filled with a powerful desire to cup her underparts in it and lose myself in a fantasy whereby I held a young girl by her clitoris.

Instead I began to stimulate Liliane with exquisite gentleness. It was bliss. The pleasure and excitement mounted as I worked magic with her vulva and we fell silent as her sumptuous swollen clitoris throbbed under my fingers. I fought for self-control, to keep the spell going and not overdo the pleasure and so bring it to a premature conclusion. But though I restrained myself, keeping the pressure feather-light, she came. She allowed herself to come. She gave way to passion, shuddering in release all over her body, letting nothing come between herself and her orgasm.

I couldn't tell how long this lasted. It might have been only seconds. It could have been minutes. I had almost forgotten my cock though I was bursting to fuck. My eyes were glazed, fixed on the lithograph done by my friend Jean-Claude, but I saw nothing save for a meaningless jumble.

I couldn't stop now. Of its own volition my hand began to slide back very slowly and then move on and up again. It was as if someone else controlled my actions and I felt as if I was a voyeur watching the actions my own body performed. I was in a wonderful dreamlike state, separated from myself and watching myself make all the right moves. Slowly, lingeringly, I ran my fingers along the wet edges of the big outer lips of her cunt. Then I sampled the inner lips surrounding her oozing vulva which soaked the material of her panties, even staining that pale skin-toned dress with its delicate blue and red needlework. Through all the folds of material I could feel the heat of her come, loving and powerful, and I gently released her fanny and sought again those shapely welcome mounds, the flesh of her arse.

My fingertips remained in her groin, between her straddled legs. Quite by chance I did something there with my nails and knuckles that was so good it made her groan deeply in her throat and in its turn this aroused me immensely. But I wasn't asking any favours for myself yet. Instead, I kept my third finger stiff as a ramrod, determined to do the right thing and make no mistakes.

I adored how she offered herself to me with open and loving trust. The great spread of her legs turned the crack between her cheeks into a luxuriant valley from which peeped the wrinkled cavern of her arsehole. It was pointing at me with infinite sweetness. I was in an agony of arousal and I pressed closer and closer. She shook slightly and made a small imploring noise. My finger thrust into her with little stiff movements. In response she pushed herself harder against the wall and pouted her bottom even more so that she could take maximum advantage of what I was doing to her and at the same time get the message clearly across – she wanted more. She wanted to be violated in that sauciest and naughtiest of places. If the police hold an official list of erogenous zones, the arsehole should certainly be well up it.

What about my cock all this time? It had been ignored for long enough and now was able to take its rightful share in the excitements and titillations of the evening. I had a good right hand free and I was using it to good effect. I was playing with myself through my trousers – the relief was heavenly.

My left hand continued to play at exploring. It surmounted her cheeks and rested there, enjoying its taste of her curves whilst I remembered an incident from my youth. I had learned my love and fascination for the female rear from a little girl who had invited me into her knickers long ago and been content to allow me eagerly to explore what I found there. Happy days! At last I was able to relive them. I could do anything I wanted, anything, with Liliane.

I ran my hand slowly up the incurving plains of her back, savouring what I found under my flattened palm, until I reached the sweet femininity of her shoulder blades. I found the nape of her neck. Her head fell forward into her arms and then she raised it again and bent it right back. Her eyes were closed, her tongue caught between her teeth. I worked on the nape of her neck, caressing and manipulating its sensitivity. I plunged my fingers deep within the mass of her hair and wrapped it around my fingers till it was tight. She began to groan and sob, hardly more than I was doing myself. My right hand jerked to and fro. My left was buried deep in her hair. For her part she shook and trembled and writhed her hips, ecstatic with excitement.

I began a reverse journey, making a slow and unhurried descent of her back. Her groans became urgent and imploring. I had witnessed her in the throes of orgasm when she was wracked by sensuousness and desire. Now she was pleading with me, waiting, panting with need. As my hand went uncontrollably back into that inviting spread of arse, she stifled a genuine cry of relief.

I had been quite casually bringing relief to myself, hardly thinking about it, working my right hand to and fro in a mechanical fashion. Suddenly I collapsed on to my knees and with a supreme effort let go of myself. With two hands I grabbed Liliane and pulled her tight against my face. Drums beat in my chest. With a desperate and yet tender eagerness I rained kisses on her buttocks through the double layer of silky material. I longed to abandon myself to violent greed and obscene lust but I contained it, giving way only to tenderness as I covered her bottom with kisses such as one girl might give another.

I kissed and I kissed till my throat was stiff. My lips were swollen with passion, and still I sucked at her and nibbled and bit at her using all my considerable skill. Without me touching myself and without me even looking at myself I began to feel a mighty presence, hugely erect, hot and fierce, climbing to my waist.

I was lost in my private world with no idea what she might be thinking or feeling. I gave myself up utterly to the sensual delights of her sexy bottom. Is there such a thing as selfishness at such moments? I don't think I was doing anything that took away one iota of self-respect from Liliane.

I was slowing, relishing her flesh, savouring her. I twisted my head a little and found I could kiss hungrily at the lips of her fanny though the material of her dress still separated us. It didn't bother me any more. I began to suck from the side to taste more strongly her juices.

I found I was recovering my sense of hearing and generally calming down somewhat. I realised that Liliane, on the other hand, was purring, almost trilling, and making sweet humming noises. To my surprise I began to feel a little glutted. I was still on my knees so I sat back and had a good look. It was as if I kissed her and fucked her now with my eyes alone. She was captivating. I began to stroke my stomach, my whole sexual region and by moving a little to allow myself access, I caressed the inside of my thighs.

She understood immediately what I was doing. She had sung to me a song of the delights of physical love; now this turned to a shout of overwhelming, profound, cerebral pleasure. I discovered an idescribable intellectualised stimulation in repeating to myself that here was a girl breathless with excitement because I was masturbating myself whilst feasting my eyes on her bottom.

She began to wriggle her hips this way and that as provocatively as she could. It became a simple backwards and forwards movement as if she was fucking. She would spread herself wide and then shut herself suddenly, catching her dress in the crack. Each time she split herself apart, I felt a shudder of incredible pleasure.

I didn't let things go on too long like this because it was plainly uncomfortable for her. Yet there was a funny side to it all. A woman comes back to a man's flat. She leans against the wall and gives clear signals that she's hot for it. The man is so overwhelmed that he falls over in admiration. Nothing's been undone, no clothes have been loosened and all the lights are still on. With all that's happened, they are still nowhere near penetration.

I couldn't help it. I was thrilled at the wonder of it. I murmured to myself, scarcely aware I spoke aloud.

'Life's marvellous . . .'

I got back on my knees and grabbed her thighs from behind. I was fiercer and more aggressive now, using my mouth as an engine of love to mount a savage attack on her backside. She groaned afresh at my outburst of passion, panting, finding the act of breathing difficult. I gave her all I could, all I had. My tongue was dry from its assault of her clothes and I began to fight through to her panties to get at her arsehole. I wanted to suck and probe it for all I was worth.

I moved up her back softly but I didn't release her fanny. Nothing bothered me now and I felt no discomfort even though I was bent double over her. My lips gained strength. I went on and on kissing her from tip to toe, arousing her totally, over her whole body, leaving not a square inch unaroused, unexploited, unsensitised. All her flesh was erotically excited and now I got up and took her in my arms, pulling her away from that wall and making her lean instead against me.

The first moment when we both pressed against each other was divine. It held all the profound joy of rapid relief-giving change, such as when you take your overheated body on a summer's day and plunge it into cool water, or when you come out of the cold sea and throw yourself luxuriously down upon warm sand. So Liliane and I found relief and joy in each other's arms.

Her hair brushed against my face, her back rested against my chest, her arse pressed into my stomach. Her legs were against mine and my hands held her breasts and her belly. Then she turned in my arms to face me. It was a moment of enchantment, the stuff of dreams. At last we were face to face, held tight against each other by our intertwined arms. Our mouths came together. Our greed for each other was inexhaustible. Our thirst could not be slaked. I felt drugged – I would not be able to live without this, now.

I have a dread of injections yet for a minute I had this image of a thousand tiny syringes voluptuously inserted under my tongue, in my gums and in the roof of my mouth taking everything bad away. I had never experienced the pure thrilling power of such kissing. I'd never known such a thing.

Her pussy lay at the base of her stomach pressed against me, barely an inch from my own excited sexual organs. I felt it to be somehow as pure and as right as a day in spring.

Suddenly, it was all over, for a while at least. It was as if we had been going to fuck only the once and now it had happened. My cock had other ideas in mind, of course, but we had become so elevated, so high on passion, that we needed to come down for a while. We were going to soar higher yet, but first we needed to come back to earth.

Such had been the fervour we had felt that, without realising it, we had travelled right round my studio couch, holding each other up and kissing all the time. Now we were staggering, about to fall. We stumbled onto the carpet. We fell among cushions and lay there, regaining our breath.

When I could tear myself away, I went into the kitchen. I put my cock under the cold tap and gave it a good drenching. Then I got fresh ice and put it into our glasses.

It was time to begin again.

2

It was hopeless. There was no way I could get my cock back inside my trousers even after it had been thoroughly doused with cold water. This presented me with something of a moral dilemma.

I didn't want to shock Liliane, naturally enough, by going back into the room in such a state. She might take me for a real overinflated prick, abusing her with my bloated manhood. But that was just tough luck. If I was going to be honest with myself, the very idea of holding myself back at this stage gave me a real pain.

Something new and peculiar was happening to me. The hornier my cock grew that evening, the less it seemed to belong to me. This feeling of detachment made me think of it as a splendid present to give to a girl. It didn't seem like something personal that I might take out from time to time, as long as no frigging pickpocket lifted it – it was simply a lovely surprise to spring on someone. Until now my girlfriends had shown more interest in my personality than in my cock, despite a bit of playacting to the contrary. They seemed keener to love and understand me than to enjoy me physically. And I suppose I didn't really do all that much to arouse their desire.

Now I had Liliane. She was proposing immediate, unbridled sex with no strings, something I had never experienced in real life. I had this second, really prodigious erection. I was almost certain she was going to love it.

My studio couch had not been made for the sake of its elegant lines but for comfort and durability. Yet in its way it was beautiful. You only had to look at it to know that you could pass days off work resting on it, especially if the weather was bad. I could read on it for hours without getting any back pain. It was not a foldaway bed, yet it was really comfortable for sleeping on, even for two people. I had turned my little bedroom into a private sleeping box. Meanwhile, with my duvet and my pillows I could relax completely on my couch every evening.

It had cost me a small fortune and I could never have afforded it new. It had frightened me at the time to lay out so much money on something that was, after all, essentially worthless, mere second-hand furniture. But now it was my life's treasure.

While I had been out of the room, Liliane had removed her shoes and tucked her feet under her on the couch. Her hands rested on her thighs. She looked peaceful as she watched me come back into the room. I noticed that she had undone some of the fastenings at the top of her outfit, to relax more, I think, not to turn me on. From where I stood in the doorway I could see that she had also reglossed her lips heavily. That made me think. Her bag and jacket were still in my friends' apartment. That lipstick must have been deliberately slipped into her pocket. Was she making up freshly to leave my flat? No chance. She wasn't planning to leave.

I walked forward with a glass in each hand and my cock flagrantly sticking out from my trousers. She didn't see it, not immediately. It was almost invisible from where she was sitting. Then I came into view with my weapon up for all the world to see. It stood at roughly the same level as her face.

My whole body was shaking and I broke into a cold sweat. Normally this would have disgusted me but now I found it delicious. After years of torture I could finally be myself, cocksure, and I felt all the relief of the criminal who gives himself up to the police, unable to bear a life of dissimulation any more.

She sat there, her facial expression at odds with the repose in her body. She was drawn, her complexion pale. Her face twisted a little and her lips parted slightly as I came close and her dark red mouth was the colour of my prick swinging heavily before me. I could have turned down the lights and put on some music, made up the fire. But it wasn't worth it. This wasn't the time. I didn't have to create the right atmosphere. We were both deep in continuous fantasy and desire had entered the room as I was shortly going to enter her body, if my luck held. There would be no holding back this time. I would go all the way.

She looked at my cock. Hardly anything seemed to change in her. She wasn't interested in me any longer, as a person or in how I looked, what I meant. Her full attention was concentrated on that thing dangling in front of her, so close that it was warmed by her breath. I could see that she was willing herself to stay calm, to keep her breathing steady. My cock was like some half-seen phantasm. She wasn't quite sure it was real. Maybe she felt she could trust the generosity of the outside world more than the riches of the vision before her.

I felt all the mysterious, dull, heavy pleasure of such an occasion. She stared fixedly at my cock in such a way that I was all of a sudden reconciled to the frustrations of my life, of myself, even though that sounds exaggerated and fantastical. My sole talent was for mixing drinks. Liliane came to my help just when I needed it. She straightened her back and without raising her eyes she held out her hands. She took both of the tall, misted, icy glasses and held them to her breasts. The material of her dress became wet. Her nipples jutted proudly as if they were naked. Lust and the cold wet glasses made them swell. It was just the effect a man longs to have on a woman when he smiles at her. Liliane's firm breasts began to quiver as her nipples bulged tight and full, as tight and full as my cock felt to me. The wet material of her dress was distended over her swollen breasts and it could barely contain their fullness.

She sat with her shoulders thrown back, gently rolling the glasses to and fro across her nipples. She was smiling. What she was doing to her two breasts was just as sexy for her as the sight of my rampant cock. She had eyes for only three things and those three things were obvious.

A little time had passed. Now we sat together, both with our mouths gaping open, panting. We had kissed frenziedly, ecstatically, drinking each other's saliva. Though I had put extra mineral water in our drinks, anticipating the cooling sensation of the bubbles rushing down my throat through the fresh bite of alcohol, I had now gone beyond thirst. What we had done together left no place for dryness. Liliane gave me back the glasses, both still full. I took them mechanically. I didn't want to drink. What I needed instead was to know what Liliane would do with her free hands.

She did just what I wanted. She began to masturbate herself with exquisite gentleness, using just the tips of her outstretched fingers. My eyes sucked in the sight of her pouting breasts outlined in wet clinging silky material.

It was incredibly lewd. Their rich protruding firmness tantalised all the more because it expressed her inner state of sexual heat.

She splayed her fingers and arched her back, offering herself in gross invitation, her breasts straining before my face as my cock bulged before hers short ago. She breathed slowly and deliberately, in and out, making them quiver and dance before my dazzled eyes. I ran my tongue over the edge of my teeth and wetted the inside of my lips.

I set the two glasses down on the carpet. I removed my shoes and half-sat on the couch with one leg tucked under me so that I could face her. She looked down at her tits, first at one and then at the other, but she knew what I was leading up to. I took my cock with its superb erection in my right hand. She twisted towards me, her dress falling open at the neck.

At last I could see her breasts bared under my hot gaze. Wet material still clung to them as they strained free, caught on the long elastic nipples that first bent under the pull and then sprung free, jutting out towards me. We came together, slowly, with infinite care, as if this was the culmination of some long, carefully-worked out plan. I was going to caress her tits with my cock even as her tits caressed me.

Our two heads bent together in complete solemn silence as we settled to our task, for all the world like a couple of schoolchildren sharing a homework assignment. We both wanted to see. Liliane's mass of hair got in the way and I leaned back a little to give her a good view. Yet she was relying on me. She cupped both her breasts in her hands and presented them to me with deliberation. My eyes fell to myself and I saw the sex of a man for what it really was, an instrument created and designed for the purpose of caressing a woman. I stroked it down her breast and up again. I brushed her skin gently with the head of my prick and then I pressed it hard into her yielding roundness. I rolled it against her and frotted it in her cleft. I was rough and gentle by turns. Whatever I did for the one breast, I did again for the other. Her powerful elastic nipples were strong enough almost to hinder me and I beat them with my glistening tool. It was slippery now, drooling slightly in the excitement and this caused her to breathe unevenly, gasping and whistling her breath between her clenched teeth. She was losing her self-control but her breasts never for a moment lost their proud demanding firmness.

It was becoming time to pay some attention to my cock. Liliane had already devoured it greedily with her eyes when it had jutted from my trousers. She had been distracted by the cold glasses and her erotic byplay with her tits, putting this first even as she had put first her enjoyment of my tender assault upon her arse when she pretended to examine the lithograph on my wall. Each part of her was being surrendered in its turn. Her abandonment was total, overwhelming. It was an incredible evening for us both.

Then she must have remembered that print with its tiny depiction of joyous copulation because suddenly she let go of her tits and crossed her hands behind her head. I wanted more. She dropped her arms and crossed them behind her back. It was what I had been waiting for. Her breasts thrust at me, falling forwards out of her dress. A barrier broke, a mysterious line was crossed, my sexual life moved onto a new plane. Doors were opening for me promising new heights of adventure and experience.

Never had a woman exposed herself so to me. I had never seen a woman so openly given over to randiness. She wasn't doing this to turn me on. She was turning herself on, feeding her own flame of desire by thrusting herself at me. I wasn't going to forget this. Never again would I put up with glimpses of half-covered tits. Never again would my cock be too shy to exhibit himself gloriously and fully.

Her breasts had a rosy blush like someone shamed at being caught out in dirty thoughts. I longed to kiss them. They would live forever in my heart, an intimate part of my future sexual life.

I rearranged myself on the couch so that I was comfortably sitting on my thighs facing Liliane. I kept my knees wide apart with my cock hanging loose and made Liliane nestle between them. Lightly I scratched her breasts with my nails. I spread my fingers. I cupped her breasts. I traced designs on them. I teased them and frotted the ends of her nipples. I was like a camera recording every image, to gloat over for ever. I longed to love her, to fall in love, so that I might keep her and have her for the rest of my days.

Yet I can hardly remember her face, now. It didn't conform to my personal notion of romantic good looks, of course, and I made sure I didn't look at it too often and distract myself from the action. I couldn't bear to miss anything of what we did. It was all vital. It was all magic. We were heading in a certain direction and I was making sure we didn't lose our way.

I planned the scene that followed. I measured her tits with my hands and then I let them go. I didn't lose sight of them, though. I put a hand on her shoulder. Actually, I was the one who was in need of comfort and protection, of encouragement, but I didn't do any asking for myself. As long as she kept her arms crossed behind her back, I had what I wanted – those provocative, out-thrust breasts.

I opened further the top of her outfit so that I could touch her naked shoulder and the base of her neck. I laid my open palm against her vulnerable exposed neck and pressed with extreme gentleness. I wanted her to know that this was for me. She made a tiny noise in her throat, a slight gurgle as she caught her breath.

With my other hand I began to masturbate myself with long sure strokes right in front of her, making sure she could see what I was doing. I frigged myself as if I was alone and masturbating in front of a dirty picture. My enormous prick was more than ready for this and as I worked myself I was deep in a fantasy world. The wonderful sensations from my prick coupled in my head with old obsessions that had always centred on a girl as obsessed as myself, obsessed with sex and lust and moments such as this, when desire demanded satiation. No longer was this a haunting image dwelling in my fervid imagination. She was here, in person, made tangible, hot and aroused and under my hand. The dreams dreamed in lonely masturbation had become reality.

I searched for some physical way to show how she was taking control of me, that it was she who licenced me in all things, and allowed me free rein to do as I desired with her breasts. This is the most beautiful gift from a lover, the gift of freedom, of self-exposure. The naked revelation of hunger and sexual thirst is so profound that we rarely permit it, even to ourselves.

I saw that she was giving way to the excess of her emotions. Two or three delicate pearly tears rolled silently down her cheeks. For a moment I thought it was all over and that her tears came from some profound sudden grief, the sort that suddenly attacks those of us sensitive to the human condition. Such heartache routs out desire and strikes it dead.

She quickly reassured me. Though she wept and breathed heavily, she began to roll and twist her upper body, lifting her shoulders in turn and straining her breasts forward at me, unable to wait any longer. *Hold me, Hold me. For Christ's sake, take me. I'm begging you!* Her words were crazy. *Fuck me. Suck me. Make me come. Look at me. Can't you see what I need?*

When excitement is at this pitch and a turn-on in itself, sex is like a runaway train. Mere words fall flat.

I watched her sob as she orgasmed. She wasn't sad, to my mind. She was weeping at the beauty of the thing she had striven so hard to achieve. She might have had her little flaws, certain heavinesses among the lovely openings of her feminine body, but I found her quite as beautiful as all those women on advertisement hoardings trying to part me from my money. Yet I don't think she believed in her beauty. She wept and shook as if racked with forbidden feelings. The most beautiful thing of all is to be oneself.

She wept for the long-lost Liliane, the young girl who had yearned to be admired and desired and treated as sexy by all the boys. Her weeping was a salutation to the passing of time with all its petty obstacles. Her weeping acknowleged the new Liliane with this new-found freedom from sexual restraint and inhibition. With this thought came the knowledge that it was going to be fun, it would be glorious and gay, and at last she was able to laugh her tears away.

At least, that's how I saw it. She had the most ravishing and least boring tits I've ever seen. I bent down for a better look, never stopping my furious masturbation of myself, with my other hand steadying me on her shoulder. She continued to twist her body with abandoned freedom. And now I, too, was giving way to lust. My body twisted but my torments were not designed to arouse but rather they were the manifestation of the intoxications of masturbating in front of a lovely and desirable woman. I didn't have to work my hand up and down – my hips were jerking uncontrollably in my frenzy and doing the work for me.

For the first time that evening my clothes were getting in the way. I wanted them off now like I had wanted my prick out earlier in the evening. It was getting kinky to stay dressed. The right thing would be to strip naked.

I was confused, of course. I couldn't handle what was happening. Naked or not, we had been fucking in one way or another for over an hour. I had knelt and stood, I had masturbated us both, I had made love with hand and mouth. It was all fantastic, beyond words. So we moved into a new phase. Our eyes met:

'Tell me what you want.'

'No, you tell me.'

'No, you tell me.'

That was enough for the moment. What we both wanted was the other's orgasm and so we could trust each other. There was no problem.

I straightened my knees and released my cock, letting my arms hang loosely. In her turn she allowed her shoulders to relax and brought her arms forward. Then she gently lifted up her dress a little so that she could get at the sleeves. This covered up her breasts, of course, but any frustration I felt had moved to another plane. I was out of my head, beside myself, beyond normal experience.

With delicious, controlled care she undid my belt and unbuttoned my trousers to reveal my belly and balls. The first she clawed gently, the rest she eased out into the open until they swung free. But it was my cock that fascinated her. She stared hungrily at it, every so often raising her face to look intently into mine:

'You are at my mercy . . .'

'You are my sweet and over-sexy boy . . .'

'You will melt under my tongue . . .'

'I'm going to stir you up and turn you inside out . . .'

'Every thrust, every spasm you have will be for me . . .'

'I'll make you burn all night . . .'

She must have been very experienced in all the different kinds of encounters between a man and woman, yet still I felt that until this night she had never really thrown off the chains of inhibition, never felt the true sexual freedom to dare and do all. It takes time and opportunity to learn how to give and how to take, to learn how to do it without pomposity, without striking attitudes, and without being afraid. This seems incredible: the ultimate in physical intimacy demands true wisdom of the mind.

There is nothing like indulging yourself in the good things of life to make you lust for them more and I was already certain that what I was learning with Liliane would make all my carnal adventures hereafter something new and special. And when I next fell in love, it would be something fabulous, an enchantment. Perhaps, after all, it doesn't take a whole lifetime to understand the purely physical side of love, even of great love.

She began removing my clothes and I stretched myself beside her among the cushions. I lusted to throw myself at her barearsed but still with my little white ankle socks on. I didn't need to hang on to my dignity and worry how I looked. I'd gone beyond all that.

She knelt before me, between my legs now, and began to work my trousers down. At this point of no return she had no modesty and showed no sign of shame at revealing her lust for me so clearly. She had sipped my wine. Now she longed to get drunk on me. I lifted up my hips but kept my hands out of the way. This was her job, I wanted her to do it. For a moment she left my underpants on but once my trousers were off and chucked aside she took hold of the waistband of my shorts and began to ease them down. They slipped over the curve of my backside. They slid down my thighs. She worked them lingeringly over my knees. Then, with a sharp tug over my feet, they were off. I shut my eyes in ecstasy and felt her move her weight onto my feet to pin them down. Her hands slid up my thighs, between them, pushing them further apart. My heart pounded in my chest and I would have wagered my lovely couch that she could hear it too.

I knew now how she loved to do things in slow motion, drawing out the pleasure to the point of insanity. I watched her as if in a dream, not trying to understand anything but simply saturating myself in the performance of everything I had secretly yearned for so long.

The desire to watch, something I had enjoyed since I was a child, was joined by a new feeling. I had a fantasy that she felt with me the sort of tension that a young man gets when he comes up against a tart, at once repelled and yet attracted. I'd always considered this impossible for a woman for the simple reason that she doesn't have access to pornography in the same way as a man, at least not pornography designed specially for her. But now I realised that the essence of the human condition is to put oneself in someone else's shoes – then one can achieve one's heart's desire.

I opened my eyes again. She proved my

point. As I had spontaneously masturbated myself at the revelation of her exposed, jutting breasts, now she began to arouse herself, masturbate herself with her hands and her arms, up and down, around and around, through that soft, slippery, revealing, teasing costume. She broke off to put one of my ankles up over the back of the couch. My other leg she pressed against her breasts. She put my hand around her thigh so that we were woven together. Then she went back to her self-arousal. It was as if her whole body was her vulva. She stimulated every square inch into electric sensuality.

At that moment I felt there was a difference in the lust she was feeling and that felt by a young man – me – shamelessly watching. Here was a woman totally open, in orgasm. Yet her face held a hint of regret. Something was missing. My gentle compliance and continued erection were not enough. It seemed that the male body while it remained passive could not thrill enough.

I was right. As my hand took hold of my cock to renew the fantastic sensations it felt when I worked it, gloriously enhanced by the presence of my willing accomplice, her face changed. The slight flushing of her irritation vanished. Her expression calmed and softened in relief. Neither grave nor gay, she was at peace.

We spend so much time asking when no one can hear. Suddenly, from out of the blue, we get offered what we secretly long for. There's no need to fantasise. It's really happening. Face muscles stop obeying the rules – you can't even smile any more. Sexual bliss can go no deeper. Contact is vital. Without it, our lives are poor, deformed, feeble and obscure – we move like sleepers.

At that dinner party on the second floor I had thought Liliane false and artificial: now she was a pale, elegant young woman, serene in her sexual tension. She wasn't my usual type at all on the surface, not particularly good-looking even, but her honesty seduced me. It was her genuineness that got to me. Normally I went for the simple, charming types at table, yet when I got them on my couch they were always the sort who turned out to be both calculating and conventional.

So how did I seem to her, when she stripped me? Immature and hopeless, I should think.

I didn't trust my face anymore. I had to let it be seen or sink myself in amongst the cushions. I couldn't control it. I was in turmoil. It must have shown in my shaking lips, my flushed cheeks, my feverish eyes and my damp forehead. Emotionally and physically I was stripped bare. Yet I wasn't shamed or embarrassed. I loved it.

I still wore a t-shirt and my blue jumper. They were no protection from her or from the flame in her eyes. I was frightened to let her see how it had excited me to masturbate with her watching. Torn between lust and terror, it was no wonder I couldn't control my face.

I could see she was revelling in what was happening but I was frightened she might find something obscene in my face or my groin. I wanted her to be shocked. I wanted her to be indecent – that was great, I couldn't ask for more. But we had been brought up as Catholics and obscenity is strictly condemned. In a luke-warm way, this kind of condemnation recommends everything else and by everything else I mean women. Nothing in my religion could make me see women as obscene. The more openly they exhibit themselves for me, the more I find them beautiful and good, poetic and inspiring. The obverse isn't true, of course. Sexual arousal is a different thing for women. The obsessions of men don't do for them what the sight of their bodies does for us. But that night, thanks to Liliane, I found the holy road to a woman's lust. I took it with my thighs apart and my cock in my hand.

Shamelessly she fondled her clitoris, her slit, and by bringing her hand round from the back, she entered the valley between her buttocks. She didn't keep to any one thing – her hands were everywhere, in her hair, in her ears, all over. She crossed her arms to stroke her shoulders and massage her neck. She uncrossed them and held her breasts, rubbing and squeezing them violently, far harder than ever I would have dared. She caressed them, she cradled them, she masturbated them in ways I knew nothing about and then she lost patience and tore open her dress and plunged in her hands, working with her fingers as if something precious was hidden in there, some long-held dream or desire.

What set her free, unchained her desire, liberated her, was me. Each time she looked at me her eyes flamed to see what I did. She couldn't have foreseen it, she couldn't have known I would do this. It shocked her to see a man masturbating his prick in front of her, for her delectation. Her eyes were profoundly blue, coal-dark, and they incandesced with desire as she watched my actions. She could see how the sight of herself aroused me. She could see how it excited me to expose my sex to her. She knew I wanted the sight of my masturbating prick to make her randy. The whole thing was a revelation, a bolt from the blue, one of life's glorious surprises. She would never be the same. She was going to want this again and again. It would become part of her love-making, part of the way she would strip a man of self-consciousness. There aren't all that many men willing and prepared to surrender themselves totally to a woman in the same way that they expect a woman to do for them. But for Liliane, this was how things would be in the future. Her sexual life lay along new paths. Fate was playing his part, when she asked to come up and see my flat. Maybe she thought I was a particular type, a safe man, one who wouldn't assert himself too much. It had allowed us to come to this point together. Our exploration, our adventure, was mutual.

Suddenly her fingers were at her mouth. She shut her eyes and concentrated on sucking them, kissing them, licking them and then, with them saliva-wet, she frotted her breasts. She continued with eyes open, adoring her fingers with her mouth, a lipstick-red slash invaded by those copulatory fingers. Her mouth hung wide open, I could see her tongue writhing, and the sight of her blood-red nails within her blood-red lips thrilled me. Her mouth foamed and I thought of other places foaming with sexual juices. Her lipstick smeared, her fingers became stained, her breasts were love-marked. Then her breasts began to suffuse with sexual heat, flushing darkly in a rage of lust and excitement. All her skin glowed dark and fiery and then she caught sight of herself in a mirror on the far wall. She actually blushed. Her tongue was a great swollen organ protruding from her mouth, quivering. All her lower face was blurred with lipstick as if love-bitten and sucked to gross excess. I found it indescribably beautiful.

My cock was extraordinary. It ached with joy. My hand shook on it in a dance of lust. A pearly drop oozed from it and it glistened with the self-made lubricant as I smeared it all over. I could hear myself groaning, whimpering like a child, given over to greed and bliss. I had known exciting sex before but then it had been a depressingly inept affair with me an ignorant novice, crude fucking only. It was like snatching at half a stale sandwich when there's a banquet spread, if only you knew how to find it.

This, however, was getting better and better. I could have spent the entire night ejaculating in this position, slumped back with one leg over the back of the couch and the other caught up by my right arm. Still I had on those little white ankle socks and my blue jumper. Gloriously, there in the centre of me, was my most beautiful part, my cock, ethereal, at once gentle and hard, incredibly huge and swollen, my own erect member held by my left hand in front of Liliane.

Suddenly I realised that I, too, wore lipstick. That time I had been in the kitchen trying and failing to get my bloated cock back into my trousers, she had recoloured her lips. Why? Because our kissing and mouth to mouth lovemaking had eaten most of what she already wore away. Momentarily I tasted her again in my mouth. It was incomparable. And quite certainly I was stained with what she had then worn on her lips. I became heated and felt myself blush with shame.

I think she knew what went through my mind. She knew and she enjoyed knowing and she didn't care if I knew that she knew . . . Ripples of excitement continuously shook her like waves running up a beach. I didn't know why, but something was arousing her again. I twisted my head and wiped my face on my knee. I wanted to soften the effect of any lipstick there might be.

For a while she forgot her glowing rosy breasts. They swung free as her hands ran voluptuously down her body, over the sweet rounded mound of her stomach and on and down onto her thighs. She arched her back, pushing her body forward over me. Her hands slid up her thighs, hesitated, and then with her fingertips she began to nuzzle and tease at her slit.

She began to stimulate her clitoris into quivering erection. She rose slightly on her knees and pushed her hands on and round under herself so that she could finger her rear and make her anus throb in concert with her pussy. This had the effect of clamping her arms tightly to her sides which pushed her breasts together, trapping them so that though they could not swing dizzily about before my feasting eyes, they became round hard inflamed globes of desire.

I was adrift in a waking sea of desire and illusion made real. Somewhere in my past and utterly remote from me now was someone, callow and crude, who with his mates had thought of women as two legs with a hole between them. We strutted, schoolboys that we were, bragging that that was all we wanted from a woman. That had been my idea of sex. Before me now was sex – rich, varied, juicy, firm, stiff and above all else, real. I wanted to kiss lips thick with lipstick for the rest of my life. I wanted to kiss cunt-lips – I wanted to taste lipstick there.

She didn't seem to have that strange detachment I was labouring under, as if her organs of sex didn't belong to her. On the contrary, it was as though she had thrown a master switch and electrified her whole body. She caressed herself and then suddenly almost overbalanced as she threw one hand behind herself. Frenziedly she invaded herself, front and back at the same time. I could see on her face that she would do whatever she wanted for herself because there, in front of her, I was bringing my cock to the point of orgasm. That was the paradox. For each of us to do just what we wanted to ourselves, we had to have the other one present. We wallowed in the freedom.

She gentled in her treatment of herself, fondling herself softly and more dreamily as if she wanted to remain in her state of arousal without taking it any further for the time being. To my surprise, she began to focus on me. My tumescent cock became the most interesting thing in the room, both for her and for me. Oh, Liliane – just the memory makes me groan!

I had become clumsy in my manipulations of my cock. I had locked myself into a fantasy where I was a member of some arcane and remote civilisation, one that took female captives. The male members would then display their erect penises before the bound women. The lascivious thoughts and images this aroused made me retract my foreskin erratically. I lost my rhythm. I was like a boy with his prick before his actions become mechanical, when it is still all marvellous and fresh.

Yet it got better, my indulgence of myself, better and better again. I can't put into words how my gland felt. I hung on – and it exploded. I ejaculated right onto her, shooting my sperm over her body. It was so easy. I gave it like a present to her, and as for myself, my cock entered a state of grace at the release granted to it by my hand. For this was what we had decided, it seemed to me, without us ever saying one word on the subject. I would deny myself nothing. My body would do as it willed.

I was broken, helpless, undone. I was at peace.

3

I shook all over. My whole body vibrated. I had little experience of fucking for extended periods. I lost track of the minutes, I lost track of the hours that were passing. Usually the moment of climax rivetted me so that I thought of everything as before and after, and after the climax I thought of things as finished. But now I panted and my chest heaved and there was a ceaseless susurration in my ears like the muted roar of the sea. My blood surged and pulsed in my veins. I loved it better than the best music, this masterpiece of love-making that we were orchestrating between us.

I couldn't stop groaning. I wanted quite desperately to talk, to tell her in a hundred ways how I was utterly at her mercy, unstrung, and genuinely lost in her. I was going out of my mind. But when I tried to frame words, I found I had to sigh just once more, breathe in just once more, before I could gather myself to face the enormous task of actually saying something.

So what was I frightened of? We weren't

playing roles, we weren't acting out stereotypical behaviour, we were free. I might find myself shouting out like a woman, I might find myself failing to look overcome at the appropriate moment – but did this matter so much?

I admit I was tempted to play safe by getting up and ripping off her clothes and doing the macho bit, being a Real Man and performing the prescribed ritualised behaviour these occasions demand. At least it would be dignified. But somehow I managed to prevent myself and so I managed not to mess everything up. I had just enough common sense to refrain from becoming the traditional male, though it would have been so easy. Once my sperm is gone and my ejaculation complete, I tend to feel self-disgust. I can't get it up any more. It became useless me having a woman and I become useless as a man for her. I just want one of us to get the hell out of it.

Not this time, though, not with Liliane. I was not going to put up with such feelings any more and the bitterness they engendered. No way was our passionate and luminous intimacy going to degenerate into something dirty and absurd. Sex did not finish with the act of love.

I released my thigh and began to pull up my jumper and t-shirt like a girl intent on revealing her breasts for her lover, only in some blind way, I was doing it for self-protection. The blood roared in my ears. My knees were drawn up and wide-open, exposing my cock. It was no effort to keep them like that – I was emotionally numb at that moment. I didn't know where I was and had to think very laboriously of the answer. You are in your apartment. You are on your studio couch. You are on it with that friend of Antoine and Joelle – what is her name? Ah – Liliane!

I held my cock at its root to keep it pointing upwards but I had lost the energy to masturbate. I was like a capsized ship with my keel sticking up in the air. All my most private parts were on display but they felt numb as did the nape of my neck, my temples and my ears. Still the blood pounded as I lay there with my useless cock exposed to a woman's gaze.

She put her hands under my knees and I jerked in shock as if I was in the dark and had believed myself alone. My eyes flew open and the bright light frightened me. I wanted to get up, not to assert my maleness, but cravenly to dim the lighting. I couldn't do it. I couldn't imply that softening the lights was more important than her hands on my thighs, caressing me there. Yet I acted as if I wasn't aware of what she was doing. Fear made me foolish, yet at the same time I wanted to hold myself back, waiting until I knew better what she planned for me.

She put her breasts back inside her top and did up the fastening. My nakedness fascinated her the more because she still had her own clothes on. In everyday life clothes are like a second skin, something we don't think about. But take them off and we find we have underneath a membrane hypersensitive to the open air, and a featherlight touch is like being struck by lightning. Her hands on my thighs made me convulse inside. I might have been flayed. Every part of me was concentrated on this purely animal, totally sensual feeling. I was ecstatically alive like a wild beast.

She straightened my legs and stroked the soft sensitive flesh at the backs of my knees. It was a demonstration of female love, female sensuality. I might as well have been a woman she was adoring. She was arousing me so delicately that I felt humbled. She honoured me and the fineness of my feelings.

How do we possess others? By laying seige to them? By dazzling them? By consuming them? The simpler and more obvious we feel the answer to be, the less likely we are to ask the question. My body, my poor beleaguered soul, was begging for the touch of her fingers and her lips. At that moment I would have wept if anything had come between us. She had not even touched my naked sex but I was not surprised to know that I knew she would, in her own good time. I was delivered up to her utterly and what was most at her mercy was what she most wanted. Her prolonged, elaborate preparations for her assault on my cock were more thrilling than the best moment of my childhood, when we decorated and lit up the Christmas tree.

She leant over me. She raised my arms. I was passive as she took off my jumper and t-shirt. For the first time in my life I was completely naked with a fully-clothed woman, completely naked that is save for my little white ankle socks. I could have done with grabbing a cushion for protection, but for the shame of showing myself to be so immature and coy. Perhaps I wasn't a real man. What sort of virility was it, that sought sanctuary behind a piece of covered foam? So I abandoned myself to her, with not just my cock, but my whole self laid bare before her.

I gave Liliane total freedom to do as she wished with my inert body. In return she taught me I was sexual from my head to my toes. The logic is obscure, but I believed somehow that I would recommence ejaculating, continually able to offer up little spurts of spunk. Yet I would not for the worlds have come to climax if it meant ending this incredible fervour of sensual joy.

I think I closed my eyes again. I was waiting on her, for what she would do. My eyelids felt on fire and the rest of me bathed in the glow of her sexual heat. She spread open my thighs again and I'm sure I tried to clamp them shut. But avidly she prised them apart, as if they held the sweetness of forbidden fruit and she would feast on it. My momentary resistance excited her.

She put her hands on my chest – I raised myself to meet her touch. She made her hands into claws and ran her red nails down across my belly and so to my cock which lay upon it. She bent right forward with her shoulders between my knees and her elbows where my thighs met my groin. I wished she was naked like myself. I longed to feel her, skin to skin.

Her hair grazed my body. She put out her tongue and with it she impaled me, rendering me nerveless. Her tongue was on my cock. She could read in my face how I was lusting for this. She wanted me wet and she used her mouth to do it. I felt her teeth on me, then her lips, then she soaked me, drowning my cock in her juices. I thrilled as she sucked me. I thrilled as she released me because she came straight back at me from the side and began to suck my cock all over again. She wanted to prove to me that she wouldn't easily let me go. The best place for my cock was in her mouth. Her mastery was supreme. Her mouth was wet warm velvet and her tongue an active agent for lust. She turned me inside out, my heart, my mind, my being. The pressure of her lips told me that this was right, no faster, we could do this forever. She sucked me like a young girl just discovering a man's cock can be kissed and so entranced by the knowledge that she adds little doses of tenderness and sensuality to vary the saucy brew, much as one turns up and down a light using a dimmer switch. Time lost its meaning. Liliane made love to me so easily, holding me by the hips and making love to my groin with her face.

As she bent to her task, her bottom must have poked tantalizingly up into the air. By now I'm sure that she too wished she was naked, but she could not stop what she did. Her tongue slid into the hollow of my groin. She kissed everything she found with hot sweet kisses. Then she released my hips and put her hands under my thighs. I might have been drugged, the way I allowed her to hitch my legs over her shoulders, doing nothing myself as she buried her face in me. Each time she moved, her hair brushed my inner thighs. It was like getting electric shocks.

Again and again her mouth came back to my cock and sucked it anew, as if she was holding me in a state of readiness for something even more passionate to come. Yet what could have been better than her face at the base of my belly? I remained alert, yet where were her cheeks, her nostrils, her mouth and her ears? My skin felt supple and fine, soft and smooth. My flesh felt delicate and new-made.

I kept the weight of my legs from bearing too heavily on her and at the same time I propped up my head with a cushion so that I could see better. I wanted my eyes open so that I missed nothing now.

I was right. I could see how her arse stuck up behind her as she bent to her work. I painted in my imagination a picture of her naked from the rear. The cheeks of her bottom would make a heart-shape that would come down to a point with her clitoris projecting like a little pink soldier from amongst her black thatch. If she had been on all fours with her arse about-face, pointing at me rather than away from me, I think that I might have been even more aroused than I was. Perhaps that was impossible. What I really longed to do was to see her from the back with her perfect buttocks straining under the skin-coloured material delicately traced with red and blue stitching. For years I had gazed fairly absent-mindedly at women's bottoms. Now I was hooked. I had fallen in love with a set of female buttocks. I was drunk on them, dependent on them, mainlining. All I wanted was to feast my eyes on them, fondle them, kiss them and abase myself to their desires.

Then I saw my cock. I got a jolt of surprise. It was all smeary with lipstick and glistening with saliva. I began to shake slightly. I had guessed, prayed that she might do this to me. It was yet another deep fantasy coming true. It was like vertigo. I was dizzy. We had gone beyond anything I might have planned. I have always had a thing about what women wear on their lips. The very first lipstick stains on my collar had filled me with excited pride in my youth as had lipstick on my face. *At last*! I had thought at the time. Now, with Liliane, I thought again, *At last*! I was escaping from the loneliness, aridity and cold that are the reward of a virtuous life.

She looked up to share with me the delight she felt in my colour-changed cock. She was a beautiful and contented animal, crouching there with her head up and her prey between her paws. She held my eyes but dropped her head slightly, tilting it to one side and holding my cock in her mouth. Her gaze was sly and alert. What did she want to know? I could find nothing to say beyond: *It's wonderful. It's so good. It's beautiful.* I began to calm down a little. I looked at her open mouth at my sex. My shaking quietened. My cock was like an old-fashioned pen dipped in the ink of her making. I had a sudden longing for music.

For her, too, all problems evaporated. Just before she dropped her eyes I saw in them her intention to lavish all that she could on what was to come next. Then, quite suddenly, she decided instead that she would take off her clothes. Before taking the ultimate plunge in the deep boiling fires of lust, she wanted to be naked.

She knelt up and released the fastenings at the neck of her dress. Then she undid the belt and released all the lower fastenings. Her arms swung free by her side. The material of her costume was so silky – it reminded me of my own skin where she kissed me on my inner thighs – that it fell free quite easily down as far as her thighs where it caught on the curves of her bottom. She leaned forward slightly. Her breasts swayed to and fro. I delighted in them as I delighted each summer at the naked-breasted girls on the beach. It was a treat usually denied me in winter. In bed, by the time I had thawed out a girl sufficiently, our love-making was about over.

Her one-piece suit fell away completely from

her body as far as her knees. Then she had a struggle to free her limbs from it. To get it over her knees she had first to lift one and then the other leg, twisting her body, working it over her ankles and then freeing the sleeves which were caught among the cushions. So it was that I watched a kind of belly dance though she also writhed her shoulders in such a way that I feared she might pull a muscle in her back.

To my delight she was wearing an exotic pair of french knickers cut high over the thigh and silkily loose. I could imagine the effect from the rear. I thought of lowering the lights and putting on music but as before, I knew it was too late. She had cast aside her dress. It was not my place to delay matters. I could not keep her waiting now.

She kept her silken lingerie on. As to why, I don't know. Maybe she had plans to remove it later, at some special moment. So much the better, as far as I was concerned. She was as near-naked as possible yet there was more to come.

The catechism teaches us about low women and I am quite certain that those alluring temptresses wore such knickers as Liliane, silk-clad sinfulness, and I am also sure that their hair was of the same luxuriant abundance as hers, unlike those virtuous women who scrape back their hair and pin it tight. And I am sure that wicked women all share the same air of wonderful self-confidence.

She pulled up her knickers tightly. The outer lips of her pussy became almost visible, bulging slightly against the straining material. Fronds of pubic hair curled out around the panties. I have a long-standing aversion to the gross swollen cunts displayed in dirty pictures but Liliane's was beautiful in its generosity, being plumply rounded and deeply divided, evoking the image of an apricot at once firm and ripe. I wanted to sink my teeth into the flesh so that the juices would run down over my chin.

She leant over me again, between my thighs. She was crouched down on her ankles so that her bottom was held open. Her hips were compressed and showed little dimples. I sprawled in the cushions, wallowing in comfort. Then she surprised me again. She leant right forward and brought her arms underneath me, increasing the pressure until I raised my hips. Instead of touching me and caressing me, she slid a cushion under my backside and raised up my pelvis. Her care of me was extraordinary. She put two cushions under me. I floated up. A sudden access of energy made me feel lighter than air.

She stood up. She gripped me by the ankles. She was shackling me. But I was already trapped by her erotic power.

I gulped. She released my ankles and caught my cock with her two hands. She made rings with her thumbs and forefingers and with them she made it stand straight. Then she bent it towards herself and launched her whole body forward, taking my cock deep into her mouth. Her mouth was stuffed full. Her cheeks sucked hard, her nostrils pinched shut. Her red lips stretched tight, ringing my cock. This was the night of my life. Whatever frustrations I had suffered in the past, they were more than made up for now. I had never seen lust like this in the face of a woman.

Her mouth came down on me. I was on the crest of a wave and such a wave! I was surfing on an ocean-roller. Total power held me up. I wanted to stay there forever, not be made to come. That would be like being dumped unexpectedly on the beach. Her desire kept me up and I was at its mercy.

There can be no forgetting that moment when my cock was engulfed within her mouth to at least half its length. It's branded in my memory. She squeezed her eyes tightly shut and cried out. My cock stifled her cry and yet it was also the cause of her sweet agony. I could read her thoughts, I knew what she was thinking. I believed in it all, now. This was no illusion. This was Liliane.

I must have disappointed many girls, one way or another. Until that day no young girl, no young woman, not even my more mature partners had been able to handle my pathetic suggestions and demands. No mouth behaved as I wanted it to. But Liliane knew just what to do. She could have been myself, the way she went for me. She did exactly what I wanted. I believe that had I been born a woman I would have been subject to the same sex-drive that I feel as a man. I suppose all men think the same. Had I been the woman that night, I would have gone at it with the same gluttonous frenzy. I would have been as Liliane.

An erection can mean misery. The beautiful mysterious desire comes bubbling up one's cock as a mental and physical sensation. You can be straight or bent. You can know it all or be quite ignorant. All you want is satisfaction but you might well wait in vain for hours, years, sometimes your whole life. Each ejaculation renews the failure.

She sucked me with abandon, wild and sweet. I shouted aloud, crying with her so that we were deafening for a moment but then her note changed. Her cries became low, piercing pleas that went straight to my heart. They told me, wordlessly, that this was no dream in the wilderness. It was true. Women adored this, too!

I throbbed with joy. What was happening was so important that I longed to talk about it, yet in some way I felt I didn't have the right to do that. I think she wanted to, as well. This was for me without a doubt the best, no, the very best there could be in the world. It could not be surpassed. She groaned in ecstasy, her mouth clamped tight as she worked my cock.

I have always felt a wry amusement at the triviality of the male orgasm at the moment of ejaculation. If the sex is good, I want it to last all the longer. That's how I've always felt. That evening, though, I forgot my tastes, my preferences, the usual way I went about enjoying the sexual act. I was learning from new, starting over. I watched her at my body and I listened to myself. I stored up what I learnt for future occasions. I would not lose out again after this. My body was all alive – even my toes were aroused. The whole thing overwhelmed me.

A corner of my mind remained calm in the riot and began to dwell on the excess of spunk about to shoot out and cover us. Only then would my lust be appeased and my frenzy able to abate. It would cool my fever, this fountain to come. It would soothe like the finest and richest beauty lotion. I found this idea delicious. I didn't realise it was a completely new thought. I had never thought twice about the quality of my spunk before. If the woman was pleased, that was an end to it. It was hardly meant for sharing.

The process was inevitable now and I was long past the point of no return. My orgasm grew in me. The final few moments stretched into infinity. Time slowed almost to stopping. This hadn't happened before. I knew all about pain being extended from visits to the dentist, but for this to happen with physical pleasure – it was more likely to be over in a flash. It went on and on. It was like watching someone teetering on the edge. They have to fall sometime but still they hang on, on the brink, not quite tipping over.

The someone was myself. I was over the edge. I hung in the dazzled air, light blazing around me.

Liliane, I have entered paradise. I am in love with the act of love. I am near crazed with excitement as we arouse ourselves to the point of rapture, each provoking the other.

No elaborate descriptions, I promise, of my first stupendous orgasm as a free man. Even to express gratitude excites me.

It was a night of marvels for me and there never was the time to talk about it. I need to write it all down before I forget. We need the written word to sort out what is worth remembering and we need it to keep the reality alive. That is what life is, what people do and think. As I go on and change, I will always have this, written as I am now.

I want to stop but new ideas tumble through my mind. It's so hard, but it has to be worth it. Nothing in my life has prepared me for such a profound orgasm. No more am I able to write of such things without being shackled by prudishness. My phrases are maladroit. I use the right sexual terms, but after that I find I have only the same words over and over again: soft and hard, real, then, we began, open wide, quickly, my heart, abandoned, slowly, deliberately, again, adoring, sure, life, a moment later . . . and if I begin to use the word succulent, I shall never get out of all the nooks and crannies and delicious wrinkles of a woman's body.

I adored her, smeared with my spunk. She even had it in her hair.

My cock began to convulse. She must have known for some time it was about to happen. She adored it happening to me. I don't really know why. A woman can turn on a man fairly easily so it is hardly a unique experience. But then I thought about it. We had melted into the same person. My arousal was hers. My randiness was hers. We could have exchanged places – our pleasure was shared and mutual. My orgasm was hers and she was experiencing a joy as profound as mine. So our feelings fed one from the other. The temperature rose. It was unbearably wonderful.

Her head fell forward over my bursting prick and she took it deep into her mouth. Then she drew back so that it came out and she could look at it, and have a chance to breathe! She never closed her mouth. She never stopped crying out, even when my cock was stuffed right in stifling her cries and half-strangling her breathing. I hear her cries still but not with my ears. They came from somewhere deep inside her and they penetrated to somewhere deep inside me.

I wanted my cock deep in her cunt when I came so that it could be completely enveloped, something her mouth could not quite manage. Yet I was patient, even at such a moment.

She knew what was coming and prepared herself to swallow it all down, allowing the product of each orgasmic spasm to gather up at the back of her throat. But then she realised what was in my mind. She adored indulging my fantasies. She knew what it would mean to me, the two of us revelling in my spunk like a couple of dirty little boys.

How did she know? Telepathy? Black magic? I don't know. This was going to be a first for me. She knew it and she wanted it to happen. There was no way she was going to stop me fulfilling my dream of emptying my balls over all and everything.

She kept taking my cock out of her mouth so as not to miss the first spurt.

Then it came. First it was slow but inexorable. Then it was a flood.

I had all the natural joy of climax. That was hardly remarkable. But there was also what I saw – long rivulets of sperm bespattering her face and the inside of her mouth. It was so beautiful. It was so good. It was beyond words. She took it all without moving. Oh, Liliane! I ejaculated all over her and in doing so I found I had never felt so good about being a man and I had never liked women so much. What I would have given, to have been in her place!

She shut her eyes and gave herself over to feeling my sperm strike her tongue, the roof of her mouth, her lips, her chin, her cheeks, her cheek-bones, her ears, and her forehead. She waited to feel it even on her eyelids.

I can't be sure now, but I think she had stopped shouting aloud at last. I think that I too had fallen quiet. All one could hear were the delicious noises, *splat, splat,* so soft, so gentle, so light, so tender and so utterly obscene.

I wanted to see her better so I raised myself up and leant on my elbows. I still had two cushions under my backside so I had to bend quite a lot to bring my face close to the magical grouping of her face, my cock and her hands. What could be more simple and right than that? She still held my cock at its base and she pointed it at herself, bending her own face towards it. She wanted the full force of my spunk. I have to say that never before or since have I ejaculated quite so powerfully as I did on that occasion. I did not wish to die of pleasure, however. I clenched my neck and shoulders with all my strength. This didn't prevent me from gripping her with my legs. My white socks met behind her back.

It comes back to me that she was a little clumsy when she held my cock in front of her face and her face in front of my cock, given how keen she was to be sprayed.

What can I say? What can be said concerning spunk lavished over the face of a young woman with her more than willing connivance? It was a work of art. It was the stuff of dreams. It would drive the imagination of a poet wild. Without words we had promised each other to make certain things come true. I thought it more moving than the vows of lovers. Had we been a film, we would have held that moment as a still. We would have remained thus, silent and frozen in time.

So it went on. She trembled and sobbed and writhed under the flow. The pearly streams dribbled over the contours of her face which was so screwed up that I could not tell whether she laughed or cried. But she was jubilant, triumphant. My only fear was that we might go over the top, go mad with joy. The pleasure was so intense, so extreme, that it was almost insupportable. I didn't want anyone to get hurt. Just being able to look at her was so wonderful, in the state she was in, and I wanted nothing to spoil it.

It was new to her as well as to me. We were both ascending to new levels of ecstasy. She wallowed in my spunk like a sexual votary indulging in a sacred rite. And she loved me watching, she loved turning me on. It excited her to imagine that this was her demand, what we did, her fantasy, and that excited me. So it went on and on.

We shook and sobbed together in the flood of my sperm. We were delirious. She began to eat it, licking it up hungrily, going faster and faster at it as if she were mad. Her mouth hung open, she gobbled noisily – and she kept an eye on me to make sure I watched it all. I realised that her shaking was more like convulsions, she was vibrating in deep spasms, she was going out of control. Then I realised she too was in orgasm, had been since my own, and still was. She had gone into climax almost unconsciously, without thought or planning, as what we were doing together gripped her mind and body. She took off! She needed no encouragement.

Maybe this doesn't seem to be so very much, a woman in climax, but for me it was all excitement. When I finally realised what she was doing, I became hysterical. I grabbed her by the arms and hauled her on top of me, throwing myself back so that I could feel her weight and her warmth pressing on the whole length of my body. She took my face between her two hands and kissed me like a woman possessed. My spunk smeared my own face as she rained wild kisses on me. We had moved into the realm of science fiction. We were two aliens, given over to alien behaviour.

I had been shouting. Now she was shouting again, right into my face and mouth. She began to work all she could of my spunk into my mouth, using tongue, lips, fingers, even rubbing her ears in my mouth. If she had it on her tongue, she let it drip down onto mine. When she heard me swallow it, she cried out in triumph. I didn't know who I was. I was an animal at bay, panting, afraid. I began to feel sick.

The truth is, it revolted me at first, what we did. But gradually I came to want it. The moment came when my spunk stopped being disgusting. I had made a present of it to her, now she gave it back to me. My feelings churned within me but I became crazy to lick it from her face and drink it from her mouth. It had become her spunk, something she had produced. Sure, I was confused. But my confusion moved me and the response it woke in me, that night we made love, has meant since that I feel much closer to women. Up to that point a woman was to me little more than a sweet cake, something I might sample from time to time as I felt in the mood. Now what I was offered so freely was infinitely richer. The two of us ate together, slowly, using our fingers, and the cream squirted all over us.

To me, no woman could see in all this any sign of love. Our madness, our sexual glut was all the more intense because what we did was nothing to do with the soft seductions of love, and we never pretended it was. We kissed crudely, brutishly. We cried out, we trembled, we sobbed. We licked up all the sperm and her cheeks were as velvet, warm and wet as the humid convolutions of her sex. I can't describe the experience properly, I don't have the words and it was too novel, but I can still remember that taste in my mouth. On sleepless nights it reminds me of her. The taste penetrated the roof of my mouth and the underside of my tongue, my palate was impregnated with spunk and the savour lingered for a long time afterwards. I think this was the same for her.

Sex drugged me, drove me crazy. I was possessed. Suddenly I wanted to go. I had had enough. I think she felt it, too. I held her by her waist. She still gripped my face between her hands, using my ears, my hair, to keep me there. My hands slid down her body. I found the waistband of her knickers. As my fingers slid under the silk she reacted dramatically. It was as though we had planned this earlier: she cried out in a loud voice – *Yes*! – and got to her knees. I eased her panties down over her thighs. A little awkwardly she brought up one of her legs and I slipped them over her foot. I took my opportunity as it was presented and sank my cock deep into her proffered cunt.

I hadn't felt my cock for some time. The renewed sensation was delicious as it slid into her burning hole. It was like her mouth, only where her mouth was warm, this was hotter. It had the texture of her spunk-covered face. I was dressing my cock in velvet, in satin, in a warm soft ooze infinitely richer than the most beautiful of clothes.

I discovered then that my erection had not vanished with my climax. This had never happened with me before. I had dreamed such a thing might happen, but never believed it possible, for me at any rate. But now it had come about. I was still aroused, but it was remote from my normal feelings. I held her passionately in my arms knowing I had conquered her breasts, her whole body. I pierced her now, impaled her on my weapon, and I would not stop till I had plumbed her to the depths.

In a weird fashion we began to calm down. She tucked my cock in her pussy like a child sucks its thumb, and so she became peaceful. There was much we might have done then, crushed warmly together deep in the cushions on my studio couch, but instead we did nothing except rest and glory in our sexual bliss.

4

Where did the next half-hour go? We didn't fall asleep but I came to as if there had been an interval, a void in my life. I felt her move and I felt the weight of her body stretched on mine.

Her lips found mine and we kissed. We were in no hurry. We kissed lingeringly, languorously, with all the time in the world. We kissed carefully, exploring each other's mouths. There was no need to rush.

In the heat of summer, after one becomes accustomed to it, one feels more intensely all the sensual urges of one's body. There was that same summer heat in the mouth of Liliane. Every sensation was heightened. And so it was in each place where her body pressed on mine. But if the areas where we touched were summer beaches of sensual heat, there was winter everywhere else, where our skins were not in contact. It was nothing to do with my flat, harshly-lit and over-warm. We were beyond familiar territory. We were naked in a rich country. Of course, I still had my socks on!

I couldn't stop kissing. I wanted it to last forever. I struggled to keep breathing through my nose and she did the same so we could go on and on. Her mouth was wide open and she kept it glued to mine. It overwhelmed me. It mastered me. She welded us together and we wanted nothing more.

It was almost perverted. There was no difference between us, no proper separation in our sexes. Our tongues intertwined much as two women in love with each other might caress, breast to breast, thigh to thigh. Or two men, lovers, might weave their cocks together to arouse and pleasure each other. We were people first and foremost, before ever we could be defined as a man or a woman. We were starting over, as if no one had ever kissed before, as if no problems yet existed between the sexes and we were so relaxed, so free from tension, that all the mistrust that normally defines human relations passed us by.

Suddenly I was aware of our two bodies pressed together and at the same time I became aware again of my erection. Had it ever gone? I had never forgotten it before, in such a state. I wanted to be in her but I wanted also to dedicate myself to her mouth. I wanted to feel her weight on me, her warmth, her freshness and her skin touching mine.

My cock was stiff. It lay within the lips of her vulva, enfolded in her sexual flesh and gently resting amongst her curls of hair. These were the parts of a woman men most dream of. The most secret and innermost of dreams concerning the most voluptuous of pleasures, the essence of the good life – these are the dreams men have of a woman's body, just where my cock now lay. It was thick and vibrant. It was so long that not only could it slip easily right into her vagina from where I lay, it could as easily have penetrated her anus. This brought back some of the delicious thoughts I had had earlier. I was immensely proud of my cock and I don't mean to boast but if I was a woman who enjoyed men and enjoyed fucking, then such a cock would have been my delight. To have such a weapon cushioned at my sex, between my legs, would have bewitched and enchanted me.

I held her in my arms and kissed her and stroked her back. A great longing began to grow in me. Despite everything we had done together, I could only think now of her arse. I longed to fondle it, to feel within the cheeks of it, to investigate the humid interior of her rear. I could imagine my hand leaving the smooth planes of her back to find instead the warm curves of her bottom. Her body was becoming familiar to me. I had been over much of its territory that night, yet suddenly this easiest of things, to slide my hand down and round, excited me unbearably. I could feel my arousal intensifying. I controlled myself. I needed to go about this thing carefully, to savour each moment. I knew the reward that lay in wait for me and I must take advantage of every moment in my progression towards the prize. I kept my hand on her back and concentrated my mind. This was going to be good.

At the beginning of our time in my flat, when she had leant against the wall, I had admired the line of her backbone from shoulder to hip. Even then, had we done nothing else, I would have had an experience worth talking about. In my hunger and desperation for her then, everything served to what my appetite and intensify the ache of longing I felt. But by now, stretched out on my studio couch, I was to a certain extent appeased and so I could afford to tread softly and take care in how I went about things.

Always I had lusted for the secret, forbidden parts of a woman's body. Yet the strength of my lust had prevented me from seeing how erotic are the other parts, how she is all beauty, in everything desirable. I made love in the conventional way and now I saw how this made me regard the back as sensual, sure enough, but not arousing. It was a feminine place but there was no obscenity in it. Never had I felt the least tremor of desire at the thought of it. Now it came to me with brutal force how not only was it an erogenous zone, but it had also the same forbidden qualities as those other places. Even on the beach one did not see it, and one would not, unless one was already in Paradise. Even there, endlessly making love, one would recognise the indefinable texture of the skin, as soon as one laid one's hand upon it.

I could hardly kiss her. I was breathing too fast for my nostrils to cope. Excitement gripped me and even she could not have understood how it was her back that aroused me, as I stroked and stroked it. I wanted to abase myself to her arse, I wanted to worship her buttocks – that was the sort of surrender that she could understand and share. She continued to kiss me but she let me breathe in our hothouse of lips and tongues. We kissed greedily, mouths agape, like in blue films where all the tenderness of kissing is cut.

I became passive under her kisses. I needed to know she still wanted me and I could not contain my groans under the lash and torture of her tongue, under the pressure of her swollen lips. But I wanted a break, a chance to drink, to eat, to rest and talk with her before carrying on. I wanted a change of position, I wanted to look at her from a distance, I wanted somehow to catch her and pull her into bed in the other little room where we could slip beneath my lovely duvet and feel its cool embrace. I wanted to dress her in one of my long shirts. I wanted to make up the fire, strew cushions on the hearthrug, and more than anything I longed to talk. I didn't want our physical joining, not just then. I had arrived at that wonderful age and maturity where it becomes possible to talk to women about sex, to talk to women about women and men, and the desires each felt for the other. (I don't think I'll have any more men friends, but so what?) And precisely because I knew I could talk to her, that same night we met, we had no time to do so. I knew we could do anything together. The understanding was tacit and mutual. But there was not enough time for everything and so there was never any time to talk.

It wasn't usually like this. When I had a girl we said the odd word, we ate something, we played music. All the time we would be eating, having a drink, talking, getting up, walking about, turning, saying something, listening to each other, when all I wanted was silence. It was with Liliane that I first felt the need to talk, because with Liliane our words would have been as naked as our bodies.

I had proved incapable of asking women for what I wanted in simple language, or of directly asking them for what they wanted. By the time we had got to that stage, I was usually beside myself with lust and wanted only to fuck. I had to get through the necessary time with them and so I used it to make love. That's what excited me.

I stroked her back. She kissed me with deliberate lewdness, as if we were putting on a pornographic display with people watching us from the ceiling, holding their breath whilst her tongue roamed round my mouth. It was as though she realised we never had to stop, we could kiss forever, that our kissing could arouse and satisfy us on its own. Our sexual organs weren't such a big deal. The mouth was quite special, not only for kissing but also for the act of love. She kissed me, her arms wound about my neck. I had already forgotten the taste of my spunk but I can remember even now the taste of our saliva, of our mouths together, so close in the cold of the night.

She kissed me with everything that she had, and for the rest of her, she did nothing. Apart from her lips, her tongue and her neck, nothing moved, not a finger, not her groin, not her legs. She kissed me with confident precision. She kissed me with subtle finesse. She kissed me with new brutality. It was one thing at one moment and then it was another.

I stopped breathing through my mouth. She gave up any pretence of control. Her tongue projected shamelessly, she looked gross, and she started to groan again though it was different from before. I, too, was moaning in a stifled pleading way. I was unable to stop. She kissed me harder but I could feel she was tiring. She was desperate, as if I was about to be snatched away from her. I don't know what it was, what she was thinking of. It certainly wasn't the desperation of love – that had never entered the picture.

She didn't want me to suffocate with pleasure. She gave me room to breathe and herself room at the same time. We both hauled in air and then almost simultaneously we gasped aloud. We weren't crazy and we weren't trying to save on oxygen. We were two separate people but we were fused together for the moment, floundering, gasping for air.

Our mouths were red and swollen, aflame from our kissing. They glowed in the big over-hot overbright room. I love my flat, I love its size which makes it easy for me to sit close to people or keep them at a distance. But I was lost in it with Liliane. We made love among the cushions but it would have made no difference where we did it. It made no difference what we did. We could have done anything. Sometimes you have to take life as it comes or you might as well give up. I think the risks are worth it – back strain, a police report!

I had almost forgotten her bottom in the pleasures of arousing her back. Her mouth served to create in me a tremendous sexual energy., It fed my roaming hands. It burned in my groin. My cock pumped within her thighs like a well-oiled piston, rigid and ablaze. Little by little, she was becoming aroused again. Her stomach fluttered against mine and she squirmed and wriggled in her lust so that I was forcibly reminded of her lovely arse and what I planned to do with it. I unglued my mouth. I wanted to concentrate on the woman's body writhing in my arms. It was full of promise, of seductions to come. It was incredibly stimulating as she ground herself into me. And still there was her rear, her beautiful buttocks, her lovely pointed arse all waiting for me like a collection of gifts. It was the miracle of Christmas. You behaved yourself and in the course of time, you were given what you longed for.

She didn't force me to kiss her. She withdrew her mouth a little, keeping it open. Her mind was obviously on other things. Thanks to what was clearly passing through my mind, she was able to find her own body deliciously indecent. This was a new experience. Contact with me was teaching her how her bottom was a source of lust. She began to lift it and move it around, as if discovering its magic power from new. It had been ignored too long. It was a part of her body where she could not go over the top, she could not harm herself in any way and she was determined to exploit it to the limit. She lifted it and swayed it about, languorously and with lubricious intent, arousing both herself and me as she did so. Three quarters of an hour earlier, I had been pierced with regret that I could not see it. Now she too felt that regret. She knew it was there, she could feel it, it was quite real. But she could not see it and that made it almost as frustrating as if it had existed solely as a fantasy.

I was guessing what went on in her mind. But I had no doubts as to whether I was right. She then made one of those significant gestures, a present for me of inestimable value. She took my hand, having stopped her movements whilst keeping her back arched. She took it and, quite the opposite of the ballerina who quickly removes the heavy hand of her overweight partner, she thrust it into her buttocks. I heard someone give a peculiar gasp. It was me! My joy was multiplied again by surprise, by her, by me thinking of her, multiplied by . . . I entered into the possession of a treasure. The joy of possession was a shared joy. We shared our lust as our hands shared her arse. (Unlike winning a fortune on the lottery, which can make the loneliest of dreams come true, lust and excitement cannot by themselves bring happiness. You need someone to share them with.)

I splayed my fingers so that she could weave hers into mine. My hand went limp as hers covered it and squeezed it. She began to move her hand so that she also moved mine. Together, in this way, we caressed her bottom. She was as far gone as me, yet she was able to contain herself. She was not yet allowing us to investigate the contours, the shape, the relief, the position of it all. She tensed her cheeks and held them rigid, firm-fleshed yet ready.

She must have been often caressed. Perhaps she had done it for herself when she was lonely and depressed. Now she was doing it with me and that was a totally different affair. It made her own backside new territory, a new place to explore. Make a journey alone, driving yourself, then make it as a passenger. Make it again with a lover – the experience is quite different each time.

Making love with me was quite obviously a

powerful experience for her. Her buttocks trembled and softened. They say we look for ourselves in the eyes of our lovers. If that is true, then surely we also can look to see our bodies at their best, when they are attracting someone else. Yet we rarely do this, as though we have no right to love ourselves.

She found herself mysterious, earthy, elegant, soft, vast and infinitely detailed; she was tempting, disturbing, alluring, exaggeratedly feminine, hungry, obscene and tender, appetising, voluptuous, pleading, wonderfully free, invasive, adorably crazy, captivating and poetic, irresistible.

Once we had experienced it, would we ever find again that fantastic and total openness, that fusion with each other that we had experienced as our mouths hung open together? I could only hope so. One shouldn't be able to live without it. Yet it was not the best of the lovemaking that took place between Liliane and me, when we were absorbed into the fabric of each other. No. The best was her wicked and tender little bottom.

We stopped all our heavy breathing and began to concentrate on our hands where they lay on the curve of her arse. She broke the silence first and she did so because of what I did. I took my hand out from under hers and put it on top instead. Hers was warm beneath mine, trapped like a little soft animal. She gave a great shout of joy and relief. She spread her fingers and let mine come between hers so that I could guide her hand as she had guided mine. I did so masterfully. Together we took possession of her, she of herself and me of her. She could touch up her arse as if she was a boy, longing to feel his girl writhe under his sweating palm, conniving impatiently in the act. We wanted it to squeeze and shake and wriggle under our touch. She knew what to do though she had almost forgotten. She lifted it and gave a lascivious wiggle. It danced under our hands. Again she did what a fantasy partner might do, that which was precisely right for me. It overwhelmed me, this precognition on her part of what my dreams were made of. She was real, there was nothing imaginary about her, and she was inspired!

I was pierced by her skill. She was such a darling, so sweet. The expertise she used on me might have been my own, it was so knowing. I understand men because I am one, but Liliane's foreknowledge of my desires moved me beyond words. Her activities moved me physically, too. She was knocking me out!

We went further. Nothing mattered but to continue. Nothing would stop us. I wonder if she remembers now how when the puckered satin of her arsehole slid between my fingers I pressed at it. It was soft and warm and tender and naughty. She whispered to me then:

'Yes . . . yes . . . yes!'

Sometimes I put pressure on her hand to slow her down, to let her feel me touching her and know that it was really happening. I gave way to the thrill. She sobbed in my ear, a stifled sound that stayed deep within me for a long time afterwards. She began to lick and suck at my ear, penetrating its recesses with her tongue. Her tongue was wild and demanding.

I was beyond thought and planning, guided entirely by instinct. I drove her hand further and further between her cheeks until she encountered my upthrust cock nestling in her womanly place. We fondled it together as we had fondled her buttocks. They were gripping it, bewitching it. It was stiff. We needed it. It wasn't just that we needed it to do its duty as the male sex organ, to be driven into the female receptacle. We needed it for more than that. It had to serve as a mysterious and fascinating object, a totem, a charm to protect against those most appalling of evils, boredom and sadness. It had the power to grant intimacy and complicity between lovers. It was a talisman and it could perform miracles. It was perhaps rather unusual in the way it served this function, but it lifted us out of the common ruck and it was beyond utilitarian usage, beyond vulgar need. I couldn't even have said who owned it, or to whom it was consecrated. Everything sexual in the two of us had become a mélange and there was little between us that was not, at this stage, given over to sex. Our organs, our emotions, our obsessions, our limbs and ears and thoughts were all stirred into a brew that would inspire and excite us equally. Well, almost equally, to be perfectly honest about it.

Our intial amazement was over. It was a reassurance to plunge my prick into its new company, her thighs, her cheeks, between the lips of her vulva. Some people are perfectly matched, they might have been made for one another. It is charming to see them when they finally meet. Their rapport is instant. Their mutual support is wonderful. They cherish each other and never again leave each other's company. In a world of misery and misfortune, they bring the blessed touch of sanity and happiness. There is a place for everything and everything has a place. So it was with my superb enormous cock. It found the right place and it brought order and rightness. I pushed its bloated length between the enflamed buttocks of Liliane – the match was perfect. Never give up. Never let it all drift. Never be content to wait or to accept second best. We have to keep ourselves up to the mark, day by day. Of course, the best place for a cock is the avid, expert fanny of a woman but once there, one loses a certain freedom of will. It is hard to remain calm, for example, and really enjoy oneself. It isn't so much that one puts one's cock inside a woman, but one's whole self, in some fantastical way.

I took her hand out from her bottom. She stretched out her arm and pulled back a shoulder to invite me deeper into the recesses of her body. She raised a leg, laying it over my hip, to offer me the easiest entrance into her.

Our bodies were now as hot all over as had our mouths been earlier. The hottest part of all was my cock. By contrast, our hands felt cool. They roamed our bodies together, interested in the smallest of details, profiting from each moment spent attentively over every part, making sure nothing was forgotten. They roamed before, behind, between, around, among, within – at one moment they were furtive and at the next they lingered gloatingly.

Her leg lay over my hip. Her movements began to slow. She reduced them all until she performed just the one, the most rudimentary and the most important. She began to swing her backside to and fro. This had the effect of opening and closing her vagina. She opened it slowly, inviting my hands to slide within her. My hands became slippery. Why? Because each time her fanny closed, I rapidly pushed my cock aside in order to insert my hand into her vulva. Its swollen lips pouted as if it was open for business for the whole night, or so it seemed to me in my masculine need.

She had the juiciest of cunts, did Liliane, succulent and edible as those of all women who adore to make love over the surface of our planet, wherever the sun shines. She could be deeply penetrated without hurt to herself, without obstruction to me. I knew immediately with her what I had within my grasp, as I had with her mouth when we kissed. There was nothing

I need do. She was wet enough for us both, her mouth and her cunt oozing the juices that would render penetration deliciously easy, enhancing the slippery joys of entering her enclosed places. It was sex without sorrow.

We slid with ease between her two places, plunging lustfully from her slit to her arsehole with our fingers, and I did not restrain myself from slipping a couple of fingers up into her vagina. I did not penetrate her far but it was enough for me to feel buried in her. I was giddy for her and I tumbled headlong.

Already unbalanced, you can fall further. She suddenly brought up her groin very sharply. It was a crude movement. She opened her cheeks wide in a hurried, desperate way. We had at that moment between us several fingers pushed into her vagina as far as the first joint. Should I pull them out? It seemed to me I should. I moved blindly, anxious to take advantage of what appeared to be on offer. Almost before they were free of her fanny, she grabbed my fingers and pushed them as far as she could into her anus.

From then on, she cried out in a way I had never heard but which I immediately understood. She yelped in a high voice like a pet bitch welcoming home its adored mistress. It isn't enough that she is full of joy. It isn't enough that she will die if she isn't instantly stroked and petted. She dances about so much that she has to be physically restained before she can be petted as she wants.

Within Liliane's arse I found a smoothness beyond telling. My eyeballs rolled up and I squeezed them tightly. I hallucinated like a visionary, a hermit beyond the distractions of the world. Inside her, I melted, overflowing with lust. It was enough! It was enough. There could be nothing closer between us, we were in it, one might say, together.

I could have considered what she might be thinking of doing herself as, after all, it isn't only women who are endowed with anal orifices, but I didn't dare. Suddenly I was shy, I was embarrassed, and yet I loved it so much. I got stagefright.

She writhed in such ecstasy that we could hardly hang on to each other, even at chest level. I hadn't been paying much attention to her breasts and now they danced before my eyes in a way that a more weak-minded man would hardly dare dream of. But I hadn't forgotten them. I wouldn't have gone without them for all the world. They were my gold reserve, in the bank for now but not forgotten. Their day would come. But for the moment there were other things to do. My fingers were doing them.

She had an arm round my neck and now it fell off me like broken rigging cut adrift. Her hand went in to her groin. She began to frig her clitoris so vigorously that it seemed to me her middle finger slid into her pussy like it was an old friend who couldn't be left alone. I loved at all, everything that was happening, what she did to herself, what she must be experiencing. I had this feeling that since she had come into my flat, I had always known what she was thinking. Yet her ardour scared me a little – she pushed things so hard. Now she supported herself on me whilst she entered herself from the front. She frigged herself violently, as if she wanted to send herself out of her mind. Our fingers could go no further, mine at her back passage, hers at her front entrance. I wanted to calm her, but not to take away from her pleasure. On the contrary, I wanted to increase it. Shyness gets you nowhere but this wasn't the time to do the wrong thing.

For the second time that night I failed to realise her orgasm had begun. I adored her lust, her joy in love-making. Now this little moment of hers almost passed me by.

I was no quicker-witted than before, yet I should have realised because her lust was contagious and I, too, was consumed in the fires. This had the effect of making me want to penetrate her, roughly and urgently, before I fell into the void. Her boundaries were down. I had to invade – I had no other country. I understood nothing. I had to protect her. I had to help her. I had to grip her tightly against me. I had to catch her, capture her, so that she could drag me out of danger. That's it. That's the truth of it. I wanted her delirious with joy, impaled on my prick, then there would be no chance I might lose her. My prick was like a fish out of water, floundering. I could feel myself beginning to panic.

We couldn't slow the action. Our middle fingers had minds of their own, thrusting and pumping feverishly. When I hesitated for a moment, she wrapped her own finger round mine and incited me to further violations.

Women's voices are piercing, so they say, but they are subtler than that. I know they have the tonal ability to shatter crystal, but though the cries of Liliane were excessive, they were never shrill. She cried out in her ecstasy and her cries were full of gentleness and tenderness, yet they were fed by her convulsions below. I could bear it no longer. I had to fuck. It was my last chance not to foul up. She'd begun it before me. It was her arse we invaded. What an evening it was being!

I had this really cerebral thrill at what we were doing. We each masturbated her simultaneously in her two most secret and intimate private places. We were men and women both. We were the human race. We were together like our fingers were together. We are thrust into the world as we thrust into each other. No wonder I was dizzy. No wonder I was dislocated by it all. What we did had a message for me, a message for the world, perhaps. It was like the wind in the trees, you think you can hear words. I knew that if we went on much longer I would know all there was to know about her, about her sex, about her feelings and her needs. They were my needs. So there was no way that when it came to my turn, I would let her down.

I could hardly remove my fingers during her orgasm. I was proud, indeed, I gloried in the aching of my arm as I fucked her rear. It ached all the way up to the shoulder. What a thing to remember! What an experience to have had! I smiled as I fucked her. She was out of her mind for the sake of her arse. She was beside herself with pleasure. Her most important thing was this. She admitted it. It had the most significance, the most meaning and it was the most essential part of her sexual life. The deepest thing, in the sense that we say deep sleep or a deep character or a deep look, is that we don't belong to ourselves. We don't have control over ourselves. Even what we weigh, it's just the result of the force of gravity. That sort of force, one we never think about and take for granted and can't escape, that is the sort of force we are subject to in our sexual lives. We can't escape it. We have to accept it. We barely recognise it, because it is always with us.

Compared to her, I still retained a little self-control, despite my excitement, my desperate cock, and my awareness of her orgasm. I worked myself a little to one side to give myself some freedom of movement. I was setting myself up on the necessary alignment, to facilitate penetration. I might have been trained in survival techniques, the way I tackled my little problem.

I got her thigh under my elbow. Then I took

her. I took her like some brute male who finds it quite natural to force a woman, and who thinks he has possessed her on the merest penetration. The moment my cock brushed against the entrance to her vulva, I seized her. I pulled her violently down beside me but I never for a moment allowed our fingers to slip out of her arse. Indeed, it was easier to keep them there in this position. A great breathlessness overcame me. I really think of myself as a considerable lover, but now I was an animal. I grabbed anything that moved. Then, with my cock sunk deep within her cunt, I lost my sense of who fucked whom, or what. I was rigid with relief. I was flooded with well-being. I shook and trembled, I vibrated like a purring cat stretched out beneath the sun or in front of the fire.

As son as I was fully within her, for the first time, she regained use of her tongue and cried out three times in succession that it was good, be quick, keep going. It was amplified like disco equipment, an overpowering assault on my ears. Maybe it was that I heard a woman out of her mind. It gave me an incredible frisson, on top of all the shuddering. My great cock filled her vagina and she shouted that it was good, it was wonderful, it was *fantastic*! I was the cat that got the cream.

Something else. I have a really sensitive cock. I found her vagina, the whole length of it, quite exceptionally lovely. Sexual aesthetics can be a pretty pretentious subject. There's lots of room for hyprocrisy and affectation. But what the hell. I had never seen a fanny more beautiful. It reminded me of my studio couch. It was superb.

We all have secret dreams where we imagine ourselves a woman, we long to know what it's like, and we also fantasise that at such moments we are with a boy. That is the only way we can know it is like to be invaded by a cock, the essence of manhood, and feel it deep within our female recesses.

I think even ugly women have pretty cunts, once you are inside. Pure beauty moves me – I get sexual excitement from it. Yet until I met Liliane, it was comfort that most interested me. I might as well have done it blindfold. So what on earth was happening to me, with her? She hadn't seemed so special at first. Now my cool deserted me, I abandoned my inhibitions and I went deep into her from two directions at once, penetrating her from the back and the front simultaneously. I hung onto her as if she was a lifebelt. I was beyond evaluating her charms and her abilities.

It was her orgasm that so fascinated me. I could barely pay attention to my own.

I was so deep inside her that when I ejaculated, it was remote from me. She sucked me in, my sperm, my cock, my loins, my whole self. My climax was out of this world.

I suppose I was a little neurotic. Up till then, I hardly knew how to enjoy things on a purely physical plane. But now I knew that my pleasure would be out of this world. It was going to come from far away, if I let it. It would knock me off my feet. It was an external phenomenon, quite natural, and so powerful that I would cease to exist.

I'm labouring this point but at the time I hardly bothered. I took it for granted. I wasn't really interested. What gave me pleasure beyond words was feeling myself engulfed, swallowed up by her and lost within her.

She began to be absorbed within her own climax. The situation was changing. She cried out still, but I could understand her better now. Still she seemed to be in expectation of something more to come, something better. It made me alter what I did. I withdrew my cock slightly. I stiffened, wondering what was about to happen.

Continuous love-making spaces your mind. You see beyond normal things. Somewhere out there my ejaculation was heading for me, at terrific speed. It was far away. Though my cock was still fairly deep within her, it had softened. It was simply a precious object, put where it belonged and left there. It was warm and safe, lovingly clasped, awaiting the right moment.

Imperceptibly, lazily, carefully, methodically, she began to slide her wet slippery finger out of her anus, slow enough to take my finger with hers, and at the same time run her fingernails through her thatch of pubic hair. It could not have been done faster without spoiling it. We came out together. It was the fulfilment of my most salacious and forbidden imaginings. It simplified things. I was hostage to her.

I didn't normally think of my climax as a catastrophe. It was something I knew about, something easy and useful to me. When I wanted to come, I came. But this time I was almost too late. It came from so far away. My cock had never seemed so long. I swayed further and further back ready to plunge in at the right moment. It was a long road but it looked smooth and inviting. I would need plenty of speed.

For the second time that evening, I looked at my cock and found it good. It was beautiful, it served me well. It was at its best at that moment, shining and deeply crimson as it emerged from her swollen, burning, juice-soaked, unforgettable vagina.

It's impossible, because we can't do things literally for ever, but it seemed to me that I gazed for ever at her vulva at that moment. I was glad I hadn't dimmed the lighting. I had the keenest eyes in the world. Down there she was as opulent and refined as if it had existed from the beginning of the world. Her hole remained open. In it I could see a promise of trust and generosity, such as we rarely find.

Still she caressed herself, her hand over her belly and one finger only in contact with her pubis. It was a touch both light and assured and it simultaneously touched me where I was most sensitive. Her head was twisted round, her face was ravaged and contorted. Yet her beauty rendered me speechless. Her nipples were black precious stones. I might laugh at my own sexual arousal at times, but I adore it in other people. I believe I worship it, as if it were something holy.

Certain moments I want to remember at leisure. In the blink of an eye, she took her leg from under my arm and put it over. I took my weight on my left arm so that she could put my knee against her shoulder. Our fingers slid from her rear and together they landed on my cock as though they belonged to the same person, someone who could not wait. Their timing was brilliant. They achieved a precision of movement and a softness I hardly thought possible. As the first jet of my sperm came out, my gland rested against her anus. None of it was lost. I bent forward and opened her arse. Her rear was hot, slippery and clean and it belonged to us both. Never has my climax been so used. It was so wonderful, what we did with my sperm, that I barely felt my orgasm in the excitement of what I could see, what we were doing. But we continued to fuck. Jets of spunk came one upon the other. I began to force my way steadily in, a little more with each thrust. I knew I wasn't hurting her and I knew, since it came from me, how profound and soundless was the fulfilment she had been waiting for.

One would have thought we stayed there for ever, at the peak of our orgasm. She no longer shouted. She no longer moaned. She was suffocating. Her mouth and her eyes were open wide as she stared blindly at me, calling me to witness what we did. She couldn't see me. I didn't know where she was. I impaled her, her thighs were up in the air and her vulva was crushed against my groin.

Gently we parted her cheeks and touched all around the rim of her anus. We could do this again, we told ourselves, we could enter here again though it would be different another time. We would deny ourselves nothing.

I don't think I could ever tell anyone how beautiful it was. Anyone except Liliane.

5

No two people had ever been so happy, so fulfilled, as us. And what effect did it have upon us? It made us insatiable. We wanted more. It is beyond explanation.

It wasn't as if we had nothing to say to one another, nor had we any embarrassment. We knew what could be said and we had no fear of saying it. But it would have used up too much time, putting into words what was happening. We shared the same needs, the same lusts, the same appetite. But we could feed directly off one another and words were not necessary or even relevant. Language can be used to stimulate and excite and we were doing this, but with an odd word or a gesture. We didn't need to construct sentences.

Another time, it might have been different. Then we might have said: 'Do it to me . . . put yourself like that . . . look at this . . . do this . . . let me do that . . . I can feel it . . . I can't wait . . . quick!'

I'm just imagining this, but I can feel it starting over – oh, Liliane!

Then I did say something. I wonder if she remembers. I am a man who likes to be alone after love-making, and to savour the aftermath by myself. I am the same after a good film. I walk the streets for fifteen minutes or so, absorbing the experience and reliving it. But now I heard myself say:

'Will you spend the night with me?'

She wanted it as well. She just nodded her head and we both knew. We were changing. We would need all our time together, if we were to emerge in the dawn as new people. Our meeting had been sudden and shocking. Now we needed time to accustom ourselves to things, to get maximum advantage from them, to enjoy them, to explore and map the new territory we had entered. As for myself, I was so shaken by what had taken place that I hardly knew who I was.

She was gay and enticing all of a sudden, full of fun. She was like a rich fruit cake, stuffed with good things, spicy, toothsome, delectable, each mouthful better than the last. Her sweetness was like the sweet icing on the cake, mouthwateringly so. Among her ingredients was her spontaneity, her complicity, her invitation to sample her, her promise of what she could do. She was made by a master baker and I longed to eat her up. Her cheeks dimpled adorably, just like the dimples on her thighs.

Yet in the romantic sense, she was not my sort of girl at all. But she had the power to turn herself from the Liliane that she had been before meeting me, into the woman of my dreams. The new Liliane was the product of my sexual fantasies, yet she was real before me. So it was that I felt as if I had known her all my life. She was my own creation.

We took a break. The fire glowed steadily in the hearth and at last I turned down the lights. We ran hot water and washed ourselves. I fetched the ice water and we drank gin. We played some music. It was all wonderful. At one moment we would sit primly and sip at our drinks. The next, we would toss off a glassful and laugh. I gave her one of my big nightshirts and slipped a dressing-gown on myself. We went into the kitchen and peeled fruit together. We hardly said a word. She smelled clean and scented like a baby, but she was so corrupt. I was tempted to involve her properly in my life.

We could not stop giggling. The shirt she wore was ludicrously big, as if she invited people to steal it from her. I thought myself rather distinguished, however, in my dressing-gown. I let it hang loose. I had no idea whether we would get any sleep that night and it seemed pointless to keep an eye on the time. It wasn't as if we were wasting any. Time plays tricks on you in such circumstances, anyway.

I asked her if I should go down to Antoine's and fetch her bag and coat. She pointed out that they would hardly still be up at this time of night. That didn't matter, however, as I had a key. She was pleased to accept. I left her doing what all women do in winter – she sat at my fire putting the pieces of orange peel carefully on to it.

I pulled on trousers and a jumper, and turning out most of the lights I went down in the lift to Antoine and Joelle's. The others had gone and Joelle joined me in the hall. She could tell I had been fucking and that I was going back for more. She kissed me as if I had been a child.

Back in my flat, I was greeted with a scene that inflamed me immediately. The minute-switch had gone out on the landing and so my eyes were already accustomed to the dimness and I missed nothing as I came into my room. Liliane was on all fours at the fire, her head down, and blowing into the flames. Her bottom stuck up and the loose shirt had risen and slid right up her back, exposing her lower parts.

Where do I get the idea from that she was the most naked woman I had ever seen? On a nudist beach, in amongst all the other bodies, she would have looked more naked, she would have looked indecent. She was naked like no one has ever been naked before. No wonder I couldn't think of sleep. She held her body in an uncordinated way, with loose, free gestures that were sometimes frantic. It was though she had made herself. And what she wanted, she wanted so urgently that she didn't care who saw, or what effect she might have upon them.

She didn't stop blowing at the fire but she twisted her head towards me a little without altering the position of her body. Now she could watch me watching her. She smiled slowly, saucily, her face glowing from the heat of the flames.

My own sexual temperature soared. I began to churn with excitement. I closed the door behind me and entered into the room where my dreams kept coming true. I became aware of her gorgeous legs. She hid nothing, made no attempt to hide anything, and was devastatingly free from all modesty or reticence. It went against the grain of things, against all we ever learn about the world, yet I could see that for her sex was quite simply a great treasure, not one to store but one to share. She might have had a piece of gingerbread or a packet of marbles. Her fun was in the sharing and she found sharing easy.

Right from the first moment in front of my picture, I had been obsessed with Liliane's arse. Not even our activities on my studio couch had appeased this longing. Now, with it poking up in front of my fire, there was nothing to prevent me from taking a long, hard, lubricious look. She read my mind. Without my saying a word, she spread the cheeks of her bottom provocatively wide and began to wriggle it saucily about. All the time she smiled at me, her face flushed red from the fire. She invited me to stare into her most sexual places, into her exposed orifices, and the sexiest place of all was her smiling face. She wanted to be part of my most unspeakable longings. She wanted the intimacy with me that I have with myself. She wanted that freedom.

I began to struggle to get my trousers off, not so easy since I had no protection on underneath. She found this deliciously funny. For myself, I wondered how come we had saddled ourselves with such a cussed and potentially painful garment. My outsize cock made the whole process even harder. I prised it free and walked a few paces forward, clutching it in my hand. My trousers slid down, I tumbled over and I let go of my cock. Even as I wrenched them off, I was rearranging the fire, shoving in a firelighter and poking up the flames. Wild-eyed, I grabbed my cock again.

Slowly, by degrees, she exposed every part of her body to my humid gaze. She touched herself here and there, turning slightly, acting out for me my hottest imaginings. I think we must all be entitled to this, after so many hours of dreams and longing. We earn the right to one fabulous sleepless night of passion when it all comes true. And when the night comes, we wonder why we have had to wait for so long.

Which of my kisses freed her? Was it a look? Or was it the silk of my cock brushing the back of her hand?

I was getting too serious. She was gay, even as she was wicked. She would infect me, too, with her gaiety.

I began to walk round her holding my enchanted cock with one hand. I walked behind her. I bent over her. I went round and round her, staring. I heard her moan aloud. I groaned myself. It was hardly surprising, considering what we were doing with ourselves.

While I was down getting her things, she had turned the music up. I had chosen it well. It had a solid rhythm but it sparked vivaciously. Its theme was being developed like the waves of the sea, gradually building up to something momentous. It was like life. It was like us.

She turned herself by degrees into a complete lust-object. Utterly self-confident, totally unembarrassed, she set herself to torment me visually and enact her own secret exhibitionist longings. She began to adopt a series of lewd positions, obscene arrangements of her limbs, spreading and splaying her body to arouse me, and arousing herself by seeing on my face what she was doing to me.

I can see her now, lying on her front with her feet towards me. She begins to shake about and quiver as if she is sunbathing on the top of a rickety old railway carriage. Then she begins slowly to raise her body, arse first, until she is on all fours. She waddles backwards in this position towards me, sitting there, until her swaying rear contacts my lips and tongue. I start to use my tongue but then leap up and ram my huge erection straight into her gaping hole. I can't not do it. I can't fall into nothingness.

And again: she goes onto her knees, spreading her legs wide apart and panting. She begins to drag my shirt up over her head, trying to get it off.

Again: she climbs up onto a chair, balancing with one foot on each arm. She bends herself forward over the back of the chair until she is draped obscenely over it, the ultimate furniture.

Again: she goes to the studio couch and before she is properly on it, falls and begins frantically to frig herself, throwing herself about as if she is in a bed of nettles. We both masturbate, but we don't do it for the same reasons. There is an intellectual dimension with me. For her it is all physical. She loves her body – we both love it. Her cunt and her face both shine. She raises her hips and puts a hand on each inner thigh, holding them apart, thrusting her cunt at me, demanding to gulp the spunk of my new-made wonderful bursting cock. But I fall to my knees and it is my mouth that advances on her.

Again: she stands and invites me in. She grasps my cock by its root and bends her knees slightly, inserting me into her and lowering herself onto me. Each time I am completely swallowed within her, she relaxes, and I feel her soft heavy weight bearing down on my member. I tilt my head to one side and she nuzzles my shoulder and my neck. Her hair clouds my face. I want never to see again.

Nothing is wrong. Nothing jars. Everything fits. Neither of us feel awkward or as if we might make a mistake or as if anything could be harmful. We listen to what desire bids us do. We do it. The apartment surrounds us like a luxurious garment and we are naked and without inhibition within its folds. Though our behaviour is the ultimate in animal nature, yet we could not be like this were we not highly civilised and refined, sensitive human beings. In no sense do we lose our self-respect or our humanity.

Life is luminous and given over to emotion. I am so full of joy I look almost anxious. My mental facilities have evaporated – I am condensed into my erection. It is all that is left in the world that is still solid and reassuring. I hang on to it for dear life. Strength flows from it into me. As long as I trust it, it will not fail me. She stares at it and I see her glistening thighs. Just to look at it makes her wet. It is teaching her things about herself, about life. It weaves a spell, it binds her with its enchantments. Again and again it says: I can make you taste heaven. Try me.

To give this gift to a woman, all I have to do is remove my shirt and display my naked organ. It is my need, freely given, that will transport her into paradise.

6

She took me by the hand and we went into my little bedroom and fucked, wrapped in each other's arms. We might have found an infinite repose together if it hadn't been for my damnably intrusive prick.

I made jokes about my studio couch and how I loved it so much, but I like my bedroom, too, though it's the size of a shoebox. It contains my double bed, a bedside lamp and my radio-alarm clock. That's it. That's it full.

There was nothing to come between us, however, once my cock was within her. It had no nuisance value there!

We lay down, we stood up, we explored every nook and cranny of each other's bodies. She spread her thighs wide and threw her arms back over my pillows. My weight covered her and I drove my prick in as deep as it would go. We kissed crazily on lips primmed and pursed the way wine-tasters do quite unconsciously, when they are sampling rare vintages.

I call it a double bed, but really it is little more than a huge mattress. I smother it with pillows, some in slips of silk. It's part of what I think of as my playboy image. It's like being on a beach – you can roll about in complete physical freedom without fear of falling off – and what you do on my bed won't get you arrested.

I penetrated her because it was the only way I could get next to her and be at one with her. I found the entrance to her body and I pushed my cock into it, up to the hilt, as hard as I could. It kept us as one person, one fused animal. I wasn't even looking for pleasure. I was looking for peace.

There is wisdom to be gained, talking to other people. But the enjoyment of another's body gives life. I held her close. I penetrated her being by penetrating her body. I was aware of nothing else and I used my member to transmit tenderness. That's what it meant to me. That's what I hoped it meant to her.

I wanted to know what she was feeling, I tried hard to sense it, but I couldn't work it out. As we made love her breathing changed, but I had expected something wilder, something more violent than this apparently gentle enjoyment of pleasurable sensations. So I was particularly moved when she eventually emerged from her trance-like state.

I just had to have more sex. Everything that had happened to me that evening was building up within me and taking my nerves to crisis point. I quivered with sensitivity. I couldn't stop now.

Imagine a cannibal coming across us then. He might have been taken aback to see us joined, fucking so uninhibitedly. Would he eat us when we were like that? Would he say: 'Beautifully warm, beautifully tender, beautifully juicy, but too much pepper, too much spice!'

She was all freedoms, all promise and so even the most banal and simple of love-making positions gave ultimate fulfilment. She was so beautiful that I could no longer think of her as real. She dwelled in the realm of my imagination. Whether I was merely on top of her or plunged within her, I soared into a euphoria that could only belong in a fantasy world.

I wasn't gentle with her. I didn't try not to crush her. I abandoned myself to what we did. My arms were stretched out and my legs were spread open over hers. We had a common centre of gravity and it was in that far-off region where my cock was – within her.

Beneath me it rose, lifted me up and then dropped me back down again into the same deep well. I understood it all. What is a woman, if she cannot enjoy this?

We became more excited, scattering the duvet to one end of the bed and the pillows to the other. Were we excessive? Was one of us over the top? The bedroom was see-sawing giddily, lurching around, spinning like a top. We looped the loop like stunt pilots. She sat on top of me – I was sitting, too – face to face with me, with her arms round my neck whilst she rocked herself feverishly backwards and forwards impaled on my cock. It was as if she was trying to drive it further and further into herself, but it couldn't go any further in. There was nothing wrong with the fit. It was just that our groins were jammed so tightly together that they couldn't get any closer.

I wriggled free of her and we released one another. We stared into each other's faces and masturbated. I mean that we masturbated each other, her hand on my cock and my hand up her cunt. But then we had enough of that. We adored this self-adulatory masturbation. We adored displaying ourselves to each other whilst we did it. But it was beginning to feel like ancient history. Now our hands roamed our bodies, perfect in their knowledge. Our actions might have been regulated, so precisely so thoroughly did we cover every part of each other. And whatever came under our lips, it was velvet.

From time to time, the one who was on top lifted himself free and opened his or her legs wide, so that they could go no further. Then like a wild animal, that one would lick and tongue the entire breast and belly of the one below. I felt that this rendered my body exquisitely fine and supple, far more so than it usually appeared to me in the mirror. And what was more, I told myself arrogantly, she hardly thought about orgasms any more. From the beginning she had allowed me to be more feminine, less aggressive than the normal male. In return, I had made her more womanly, and less demanding. She thought less, now, of her own pleasure, and more of mine.

Ever since we started, each phase of our love-making was in itself a postponement of the next. Hardly did we achieve one erotic feat, when we began to move on to the next. We were like road-menders, working along a long road. We filled some holes, but that only served to delay the filling of yet bigger ones ahead of us, waiting for us to get to them.

She was riding me, sitting astride me and breathlessly pumping me up and down with a vigorous action. She interrupted herself to lean over and with an outstretched arm she shut the door. Then she twisted herself the other way and began to wrestle with the mechanism that controlled the blind. She got the blind up. I now turned off the bedside lamp. We hardly wanted to be lit up with electric light at this stage. The flashing face of the radio-alarm was turned towards the wall. The only thing we needed to light this next scene were the stars themselves. She found it perfect, this narrow space by the french windows suspended above the city, overlooking what appeared to be the last block of old houses in the galaxy, bristling with television aerials as if they wanted to keep watch for some miraculous happening.

She'd forgotten the poor weather. Outside were no cerulean skies under which we might laze in balmy warmth. Instead there was the orange glow of street lights refracted by the dirty fog.

Concentrating utterly on me, she bent herself over me so as to protect and cover me and have me at her mercy. Her knees touched my elbows as my arms lay slack by my sides. Then she began.

She began to caress me powerfully with her tongue. You couldn't call it licking. She kept her tongue rigid and pointed and used it with muscular strength. Her lips gripped her tongue and supported it. It jutted from between them and with it she attacked my body, my eyelids, my cheeks, my neck, my shoulders. We had, in one way and another, satisfied our grosser appetites and there was time now for some sophistications and embellishments. I knew what she wanted. She wanted to have me. She wanted to possess me. She wanted to knock me about, play with me like a doll, stop me breathing, take me apart. She wanted to see how low she could reduce a man, how far she could demean and abase me. That's what was turning her on.

She wanted to work me over, put me through a mangle. If I had broken down at that point, begged to be let off, she would hardly have been surprised.

Men have nipples, too, and the hair about them is no turn-off deep into a night of love. She drew back and stared down the length of me, and then she came forward and slid me into her and arranged herself with insulting comfort on my prick. Then she lunged. She grabbed my shoulders and began to suck my skin. I hardly knew what she was at – I was out of my mind. My groaning began to ascend the register. Yet it was not like a woman's cries. It was animal.

I was soaked with her juices, not just over my body but deep inside me, where I had my spirit, or rather, that vague idea of ourselves that we sometimes call our soul. We had a need, once, to think of ourselves as more angel than beast, before we understood that the beasts could be rare and innocent and angels could be corrupt. She chewed me, she nibbled me, she bit me, she struck me blows with her tongue and I was overwhelmed by the sensations she aroused over my body. Though I could barely tolerate what she did, yet it was little enough compared to the mental excitement that was melting me down, the way a skilful lover melts a woman with his tender caresses. It wasn't sexual technique with her, it was greed. She gentled my nipples and then she roughed them up. Their taste on her tongue inspired her to new heights of brilliance. She was handling me like a genius. She had some secret plan she worked to. Each time she abandoned one side of me for the other, I was filled with despair. She used her nails on me, her fingertips.

I wanted to live. I wanted to have more. But things were getting complicated. I was tightening up inside just when I most wanted to let go. We were coming dangerously close to a ghost from my past, something that had haunted me since I was a schoolboy – I wanted to be treated as a woman.

Again she touched my nipples with her tongue. It lit me up and at the same time it broke me down with the confusion of my feelings. Instead of it being a foundation upon which to build greater things, it was bringing me close to collapse. I was terrified. Giving way to this could ruin my life. It could split my identity, break my health, ruin my living, get me evicted – if anyone ever guessed. Perhaps my irrational panic actually enhanced our lovemaking. And there was no escape for me by easing my longing and dressing like a woman. I didn't have the courage for that. My looks were a shade feminine already.

I was blowing my mind. Even to think of it now has an effect on me. Then, at the time it was happening, I felt I was adrift, at sea. My entire personality was losing its bearings. I couldn't handle anything new. It was a bit like getting an erection at an inappropriate time – it's not only unwelcome, it can be really embarrassing. I came close to fainting, there, with Liliane. That was the effect she had on me.

Meanwhile she sat there, on top of me, making a prisoner of my cock within her body, whilst she scratched and bit at my nipples. My groans revealed everything. They came from somewhere outside me, as though they belonged to someone else. The sensations she aroused in me were still thrilling, exquisite, a refinement of pleasureable torture and I have no doubt she was moved in that she could affect me so powerfully.

Sometimes she raised herself to arch her back and check up on my poor trapped penis. She made sure it went all the way in. Nothing escaped her. She stared at my breasts, first one and then the other. They didn't swell up and erect themselves fully like hers, of course, but the aureoles wrinkled and the nipples became stiff and hard. She looked also at my body hair. It did not lie as it should, downwards, the way it did in the shower. It was sticky, distorted, really quite sexy, like rumpled bedclothes, or the lined face of a roué.

With her hands at my nipples, her own breasts swung free just above me, in an ideal position. The proud swell of her bosom was like a sumptuous accessory added to the basic model. They did not even follow the line of her boy particularly well. She didn't bother much about them except to show them off. She adored exhibitionism. She offered them to me as if they were something luxuriously new and quite unusual, with a delicious and entirely spurious modesty. She adored display.

I couldn't resist. I caught hold of them and began to knead them and pummel them and cup them. I found their weight and size glorious. It made my groin throb. She controlled it all, astride me, above me, her forehead smooth and her eyes shut.

Then she bent forward and slid her hands under my back and tried to raise me up. She had me pinned at the hips and with only her elbows for leverage she didn't really have the strength. I helped her, pulling my body up into a sitting position. I loved her manhandling me. Then I was up, and her breasts were crushed against me, against my chest. They were firm and generous, and she rolled and rubbed them tight against me so that they bulged and squeezed. How could I be jealous? They were as much mine as hers at that time, even as she owned my cock in partnership with me. We shared our sex and we left the rest to fate.

She slid further back, allowing my prick to be twisted deliciously along the wet channel at the top of her thighs, and then pressing down on it with her clitoris. I had fallen back flat on the bed and now she put one hand to one of my breasts and one to the other, working both nipples simultaneously. Then she went at them with her tongue. She was too far gone to use her nails, but her tongue was going mad, going down my body until it reached my belly. She was out of her mind. She had reached the point where she would indulge any idea she thought of. She was as crazy as those who cross-dress in public, who chase rainbows, or who take up a career in politics.

My cock slid out. In the position we were in, there was no choice in the matter. I would have liked it to rest like that, in the open air for a little while, but she took hold of it and drew it down between my legs and then trapped it in that position using her stomach to pin it in place. She eased herself down my body and began to lick my navel, burrowing into it and performing wonderful warm wet wicked things with her tongue. It was as though her tongue had a secret mission, to strip me of bitterness and flood me with sweetness. I was melting, melting till there was no place hard about me. I was given over to softness, except for my wonderful cock.

Her breasts rubbed my thighs. She released my nipples at last and instead took hold of me by the hips. My cock was still trapped by her stomach and bent sharply downwards. It looked enormous. It almost reached my knees. I could see her rounded breasts which I was lusting for, my fabulous distorted cock and my hairy thighs all crushed together in a weird perspective. Everything was out of proportion. I began to feel hairy all over, especially when she rubbed her face in my groin, tongued me and smoothed my curls with her lips. She became my coiffeuse. She dressed my hair for me, only it was my pubic hair that she dressed and she used her tongue for a comb. I could feel each separate sensation. She fluffed it up, she moussed it, she blow-dried me with her breath. That's how it felt and there was no way I felt foolish.

I began compulsively to stroke her hair. Nothing could have prevented me. But my other hand I put over my stomach, pressing down with my fingers spread. I felt close to bursting. I was holding myself in.

My cock bounced, trying to force itself up. She raised her body a little and stared at it, stared at her own breasts, as if she was shocked to see a giant male member nestling there. She remained crouched over me but now she rearranged herself between my legs, spreading them wide, and using the opportunity to wriggle her delicious arse in the way she knew excited me so much. She held my stomach and thighs to her, then she eased all ten of her fingers to the base of my cock. Deliberately and sweetly she drew it upwards into a vertical position, making it ready for what she planned to do.

I put a couple of pillows under my head so that I could watch what went on in greater comfort. Otherwise this was in no way like my earlier experience on the studio couch. There she had been famished. She had fallen on my cock, quite literally, with all the greed of a hungry woman. She had wasted no time. She had been driven by desperation and she had cared for nothing but my cock, stuffed into her mouth. I could remember the look of strain on her face, the ravaged look that was nothing to do with the effort of sucking. She had sucked intensely, all right, but it was natural to her. No, the strain she had felt came from the driving force of her hunger.

Now, in my bedroom, she was caring for me more than herself, caring for how I felt. She strained to make me offload all the weight of past anger, fear, sorrow, misfortune and blight, whether sexual or otherwise. Her mouth and hands worked as if their success was assured, but it would require, nonetheless, great skill and concentration. She could overcome all the bad things of my life, before I could be so neatly remade, I had to be massaged, bathed, pampered, warmed and petted.

My cock throbbed with impatience but her lips had the power to transport it from that state into one of immediate well-being. I was flooded with relief and gratitude. Never for one moment was there pain or resentment. But even as she calmed my trembling member, I excited myself over again by looking at her. I couldn't tear my eyes away.

Then she gave me one of her sly looks. My heart began to beat and my chest heaved. She formed her lips into a ring and slid it very gently over my distended gland. At the same time she relaxed the grip she had on the root of my cock at my balls. Now she worked them together, mouth and hand, pumping my cock, sucking it, and as she did so she forgot all about me and gave herself over to what she was doing. All I was for her was this pressure, in her mouth, her cheeks, on her tongue, her gums, the roof of her mouth and the insides of her lips. I watched it all.

She did this for a while and then she gently released me from her mouth and began to recover her breath, resting her cheek on my stomach. She still held me with her two hands. She came back to herself, recovering her awareness of me, and then set about gratifying me as best she could. I wallowed in an avalanche of caresses and kisses. She masturbated my cock energetically, slipping it in and out of her mouth. Yet she took great care that what she did pleased me, and was right for me. How I longed to climb inside her mind and read her thoughts. Instead we sank together into our private, intimate world of shared fantasy.

In the other room, the two cassettes had finished. All we could hear were our two selves and the occasional train passing in the distant night. She made her mouth into an elastic sheath and with it she closely confined my cock, my cock and nothing but my cock. Now it was protected from all danger, all loneliness and cold. Though the world was but half-done, my cock was becoming the most important thing in it, ever. It was a precious and fascinating object as it voyaged into her mouth and out again.

She backed off a little and instead of moving her head in order to slide my cock in and out of her mouth, she rocked her whole body to and fro. Her energy contrasted with my lassitude. I was lost in reverie, profoundly abstracted, deep in my memories of coming at her from the rear, when we were in the other room. But when I opened my eyes, the vision before me was of the base of my cock, her hands clasped about it, her rounded mouth, her drooping eyelids (or the gleam of her eyes, when she looked up at me), her mass of hair, the rising line of her back going up and spreading out until it came to the stately mounds of her buttocks, straining backwards and linked by the valley between them.

I needed that sight to excite me like I needed the treatment my cock was receiving. She knew it. She began to lift a leg and work herself around my body. She wasn't going to mount me. She rotated herself around me using my cock as her axis, so that I could see her from the angle I desired.

Maybe I could have made do with the dim light filtering into the room from the street lights outside. I could see clearly enough. But it was too lovely to view in a dim light. I reached out an arm and put on the bedside lamp. Her shoulders jerked. She shuddered at this evidence of my greed to look at her.

She let me see her from every angle as she came slowly round. I have a particular weakness for that fold of flesh in the groin, where the upper leg meets the hip. The skin of woman just there is always so soft and tender.

I saw also, as she moved round on all fours, the swing of her beautiful breasts as they hung beneath her, pulled down by their own weight. They seemed to have a will and a life of their own. They must have been arousing men since she was fourteen, or thereabouts. Even then, they must have been well-developed. I wondered if their weight didn't sometimes hurt. Secretly I hoped that they did. It was a romantic longing, a bit naughty, as I hate pain for myself and shouldn't wish it on others.

She deliberately made them bounce all over the place, by rocking herself madly about and rubbing my cock in the velvet of her mouth with even more energy than before. Every gyration made my cock slip out of her mouth. She delighted in grabbing it again and sucking it back in. I had no chance to establish a more rhythmic action.

It's incredible how a woman is at her most elegant when she sucks a man off. I speak of the mind, not of the body. A woman with a cock in her mouth reveals her inner beauty, her fervour, her delicacy, her generosity, her sensuality, her intelligence. What of her outer beauty, at such a moment? Her face is no longer her own. She is a work of art, an old master, something to be viewed day and night.

Now she was beside me, lying on the bed. I thought she looked superb, down the entire length of her lovely body, most particularly the tip of her nose. My aesthetic judgment was suspended, concerning that nose. She was altogether a most flawless young woman and I wanted to admire her without distraction.

All works of art resembled her. It was not the other way round. It came to me that all ethics, all aesthetics, were based on what we discover in the physical act of love-making. I would have bet on it, but perhaps it remains better unsaid.

An intuition told me to turn off the bedside light. She released me and got to her knees which she spread wide. She hung her hands by her side, then she raised them and put them behind her head, making her breasts project. Her bottom had an exquisite roundness, in its two divided parts. For herself, she wouldn't have touched the light. I could see that at last she knew she was lovely. She could see it in my face and she believed it. The rhythmic flash of the radio-alarm was like the quick flutter of her heartbeat. A diffuse glow drifted in from the city lights outside and aureoled her in the night sky.

She did what people do in the gym. She gyrated her torso and her hips in opposite directions. I adjusted to the darkness, watching her, forgetting myself, and so my cock grew limp though it had been on the point of climax. She was a work of art.

I looked at her mouth. It had a hurt, pained look to it. It wasn't because of the poor light, nor was it because of the bruising it had received. It came from an inner feeling. She needed me to know, to care how she felt. I saw her upper body, her shoulders, her groin. They were relaxed.

She stretched her arms in the air whilst her eyes hunted for my cock. It waited. It knew she hadn't finished. I had come up onto my side and now she rolled me back so I lay flat and she straddled me. She looked at my cock for a moment as it hardened. Then she backed off slightly, lifted it up, and calmly put it back in her mouth.

7

The soaring arch of her thighs was lit from all around and it glowed above me in surreal fashion. She was the material from which we weave our dreams and she presented it to me not as a demand but as a gift to please me. The suggestion in her body was this: that she take me to the pinnacle of experience and bring me to climax whilst I watched her do it.

I would have kissed her between her legs for hours. I would have sucked her and tasted her and savoured her lingeringly in each private place for ever, and if I am offered the opportunity again, I will. I had devoted little of the night to such activities, far too little. That was a measure of my distraction. What she had done to me, what she proposed doing to me, what she wanted me to do to myself, would have distracted an angel. She sucked me, I gave myself to her sucking. I watched, she let me watch. That was how it was. How could I have wanted it otherwise.

She knelt over me, reversed, and let her shoulders droop as if they were heavy. Her cheek pressed against my inner thigh and she took my cock in her mouth. She might have been going to sleep, sucking my cock as a comforter to take her through the night. She had put a pillow under one of my legs to raise it so she could slip her hand underneath and she came at my cock from below, to hold it by its root.

I looked up at what was between her thighs, above my face, and felt her tongue almost sloshing about my cock. I clasped her knees in my hands to support her and make myself comfortable. I would not let her loose until our desires had been satisfied. I can't think how it was, but I failed to raise up my body a little and kiss and lick and suck at what was above it. I longed instead for her mouth – raddled with fatigue, tongue lolling and swollen lips, all bruised from the excess of attention she had paid my body. I was locked in this fantasy. Almost I longed to be free of her grip. It became the ultimate experience that would leave me breathless, conquered, sated, glutted. Yet I was all of that, already. My mouth had hung open for so long it felt as though my tongue was made of cardboard.

I couldn't bear to miss any of what was happening to me. I made myself as passive as I could, to enhance my reception of every sensation. Yet I remained self-conscious, unable quite to lose hold of myself and abandon myself to the experience I was undergoing. While it happened, it seemed unforgettable, but the most intense experience can disintegrate as it is absorbed into the memory. Above me was a jumble of arse and thigh and sweet cunt-lips surrounding the entrance to paradise all clustered with tendrils of wet curling hair, but like the face of the one you love, when you are separated the features blur and you cannot precisely call them to mind and form their picture. The very power of love, be it physical or romantic, blurs the desired object and you must begin to learn all over again.

I found it hard not to tighten my stomach and jerk my cock in her mouth. Instead, my head tossed from one side to the other and I mumbled in my frenzy, pleading, begging, muttering phrases like 'No, please no, I can't bear it, I don't want it, stop.' I just couldn't handle such a feast. It was too much for me. I wasn't up to it. I'm like most men, I'm too used to malnutrition. I never normally get enough sex and now my shrunken appetite couldn't cope. The crazy thing is, most women feel they are inadequately loved as well. That's the experience I've had, anyway.

Gradually I regained control of my senses. I became able again to tolerate what she did to me, what I felt.

She tensed her body and then assailed me with all ten fingers. I could feel her fingers, thumbs and nails. I had been stroked before, of course, over the long course of years, and I considered myself as a sexually experienced man, but never in the way that Liliane did it that night. For over six hours she used my body in a way that reduced me to a pulp. Was it talent? Was it experience? Was she the devil, disguised as a woman? Or was it that no one had ever come at me with so much sincerity and persistence before? Perhaps she knew it all instinctively. Or perhaps it was my own need, my vulnerability and hunger, that was the trigger.

She ran her fingernails round in little circles in my most tender places. I bit my lips in the effort not to cry out. But when she drew her nails along the crude seam that connects a man's balls to his arse, I whimpered aloud. I was a lamb to her slaughter. She entered the tender valley connecting my thighs to my backside and began to search it. There was a point in my life when I realised that it wasn't only girls who had dimples round their bottoms. We men do, as well. When you feel fingers and lips begin to explore and prowl within you there, it's time to hang on, grip a pillow, and refrain from howling aloud.

That was about that time I became her creature, to do with as she wished, without control any longer over my own actions and will. It didn't last for a long time, the experience, because I couldn't take it, in the same way that I can't knock back a bottle of straight gin. But for the time being I was her thing, her puppet, her doll. My subjection to her freed me from myself. I don't know if she guessed any of this because she was herself in something of a state at this time. But I hung on and I tried to show nothing of how I was feeling. Such self-discipline as I could still command, I used to mask what had happened to me. I couldn't bear to let her down, prove inadequate to what she was doing to me. We were taught as children how our soul is like the flame of a candle. Mine began to flicker madly as she had me there, her fingers deep in the convolutions of my flesh, my manhood sucked into the vortex of her mouth, and over me soared the vault of her straining, splayed buttocks, stretched wide on the column of her thighs, just above my face.

I use words badly to describe something so simple. *'You're mine,'* you read in the love stories, but it's all about a girl and her overflowing heart. It's never about the flesh of a man's arse. I don't go for the mawkish and sentimental, those dreadful romances that women devour.

She knew how she could arouse me and she did it again. One, two, then three of her nails furrowed my flesh and then ran round the rim of my anus. Desire exploded in me. I couldn't say so, I couldn't speak it aloud, because the effort was too much and anyway, it was beyond the power of words to express the wonder and excitement of it all. I writhed about clutching my pillow. I needed sex, sex and more sex – I couldn't be satisfied.

She began to massage all around my anus with her thumb, working all the crinkled flesh of my arse, whilst at the same time she clawed down my inner thighs with her nails. To my own surprise, I pushed down on her, trying to increase the pressure on my hole. I was like a cartoon character, upside down, on my head, inside out. I had no idea where I was or what I was.

She spread the fingers of her other hand, the one that came under the leg she had raised with the pillow, and using them she forced the cheeks of my arse apart, exposing as much of the skin round my hole as possible. It was satin, beneath her probing thumb.

Now she brought her middle finger into play. She stroked my anus gently but with a continuing persistence that defies description. She was loving it as I was. She knew all there was to know about arousing a man's arse.

Every part of my body she went at, whatever she did to it, she did with planning and care and thoroughness, beginning gently and working towards the conclusion, never losing sight of the end in view. She had enormous skill and she reworked me, doing a total repair job on my miserable sex-life. I learned about her during that night together, and the longer we were together, the more she did to me, the more I came to trust her absolutely. She was all-knowing, all-wise. I was always confident with a woman, but it was a false confidence. Now I could let that go. I was shy to expose myself and my inadequacies at first, but I did it, and so became free, a new man.

I closed my eyes.

This was incredible. How many times had I lain awake at night, eyes wide open, trying desperately to evoke the images of just what was happening to me now? It was real, what took place, and never could I have imagined that on such an occasion I would not stare and stare until the scenes we enacted were imprinted forever on my mind. But my eyes weren't big enough, nor were my inner senses. I had to sacrifice one for the other and I chose to concentrate on my inner experience and give up the external delights of watching what we did.

Resigned, almost afraid, sick with anticipation and longing, I waited for what was to come. I gripped her knees as if I could control her that way. She had become larger than life and I was at her mercy. It was cruel, how she had me at her will, and what was between my legs. At least my cock wasn't worried. It lay in her mouth snugly encased, warm and wet, and I almost forgot it was there in the excitements of what she did to me elsewhere. But now she slid in a finger at the corner of her mouth, past her swollen lips, and using it she began to twirl my gland round and round, batting it with her tongue and finger, running over the top of it and playing with it like a toy. Then she cradled my cock in the palm of her hand, what couldn't get into her mouth, and cuddled it.

I am sure she had closed her eyes as well. It comes to me now that the best way to enjoy something is to linger over it, to do it as slowly as possible, to savour it to the utmost. I'm not talking about what you buy or what you pay for, of course. I suppose, like all truths, it is self-evident, but it didn't occur to me at the time. I knew why her finger was in her mouth. I knew what she was leading up to. Impatience nagged me and I could hardly breathe. A constricted feeling came over me. I couldn't think straight and something vice-like clamped my temples. I was lying down, but my knees went weak, as though they were stuffed with cotton-wool. Desire was a flame in me, my face nuzzled into her cheeks, but I could not make her hurry. The only way I could find relief and ease was from her breasts, hanging below her and brushing my chest, and I ran my hands into their vulnerable softness. Their warm gentle heaviness was indescribable.

My heart pounded and I was still short of breath. She took her finger from her mouth and then she released my cock altogether. I began to shout. She seemed a million miles away. I felt her arm move but nothing eased my torment. I shouted louder. She would not hurry, she would not help.

Her finger was wet, in the condition she wanted it for what she planned to do next. She moved it to where she wanted it to be without touching anything else. At the last moment, I shrieked aloud. She plunged her finger into my anus. My cry turned into a strangled plea for help. I gasped. My lungs rattled. I fought for air. She ignored it all.

She did not push it far in at first, only just beyond the first knuckle. She wriggled it inside my arse.

She had prepared me for this. She had aroused me, sensitised me and manipulated my emotions so that I could obtain maximum physical excitement, whilst at the same time crushing me mentally so that there was no way I could resist. She fucked me through and through. I don't know whether she ever did it to anyone before me or whether she has ever done it to anyone since, but whether we meet again or not I'll stand witness to the fact that she deserves her place in heaven, for what she did to me that night.

I went mad. I threw myself about, gasping, seeing spots before my eyes. Masochistically I thrust from me her breasts and pulled her face out of my groin. I didn't mean to, it just happened. She could have rammed her finger further in. I was raving, I couldn't stop her. Instead, she took it out.

I hadn't a clue as to what was going on. I think now that she enjoyed getting me in such a state. I think she took pride in her power to reduce me to a madman with her activities. Her sexual prowess could take me to the edge of insanity. My feverish distress was proof of her potency. If she felt pity, it was of the calm, magnanimous kind. She was infinitely higher than me. She had the mastery of me. She had responsibility for me – I had none for myself. I was her thing.

She detached herself from me and began gently to stroke me and soothe me. I felt her move, the pressure of her knees was gone, and I opened my eyes. She was lifting her thigh over my head. She rearranged herself so that she sat next to me facing the window. She pressed on me and obediently I rolled over. She was my nurse. I was her patient. I did as I was told.

Now I was on my stomach she leaned over me and ruffled my hair, kissing the nape of my neck and licking and sucking at my shoulders. She slid a hand slowly down my back. It reached my buttocks, rose up over their swell and caressed them. She felt me there like I dream of feeling women, sensing their shape under my hand, pressing my palm over their smooth mounded flesh, sampling their shape and texture. I glory in the privilege of a woman's arse under my hand – so she gloried in the privilege of mine.

It sobered me up. I accepted what she did and adjusted myself to what she was going to do. I could not spoil things. I had to accept what came. She touched me lightly – it was a command. I raised my bottom into the air. I did it as she had done it, when she was arse-up in front of my fire. I made it point and strain towards her. I offered it freely. I enticed and invited with it. I did now what she done for me then. She behaved as I had done, as I would do if the positions were reversed. She had this ability to do to me what I would have done to myself, what I wanted most. She could divine what my fantasies were woven round. Lightly she ran her hand over my bottom. Gingerly she ran her hand down the valley between my cheeks. She didn't force my buttocks apart. She let them open naturally as I lifted myself still further into her caresses.

She sat on her ankles at my side. One hand came over my bottom. The other stroked my hair. She rested her face on my arched back. Then she brought it round to my rear and with her mouth she caressed my buttocks and then my arse itself. My flesh shuddered. Little tremors shook my cheeks and my anus fluttered open and closed. I felt her face, her ears, her hair, the soft silk of her eyelids and the smooth satin of her brow pushed into my rear. All the time, her other hand fondled my hair and twisted itself in my curls.

With the slightest provocation, I would have burst into tears.

The base of my prick began to throb so I eased the strain on it by lifting myself still further. I pushed my face down into the bed. Now my cock could hang unencumbered.

Now she stretched out my arms and placed them alongside my legs. She spread my legs like one opens dividers. She put her two hands under my stomach which was lifted high to accommodate my swinging cock. Then she drove in with her tongue.

She was like a fire in winter. She was beautiful, life-giving, dangerous, able to destroy, able to torture. With her tongue she united us, she loved me, she abandoned herself to me, she enfolded me, she pierced me, she fused with me, she shackled me. She was potentially lethal, but she was also compound of warmth and generosity, harmony and well-being.

So much is in a kiss, and such a kiss it was, that Liliane gave to me, to my arse, with her tongue. All sexual life is here, in a kiss. She was obscene, tender, painful – she was the best.

My knees sagged and she stuffed pillows under me to hold me up. She forced me to undergo the ultimate outrages and I felt like an angel. I spread my arms and prepared to take off. Had I been unafraid to give full vent to my feelings, I would have sobbed with the pleasure of it. I wanted to weep at the humiliations I underwent.

Her power over me went to her head and she suddenly lost self-control. She began to wrestle herself free of me and yet she glued her mouth to my arse. She moaned, stifled moans that thrilled into my anus. Her tongue went round and round my arse, hard and demanding. I lifted my arse still further, pushing at her, demanding in my turn in the excess of lust.

Then there was the most appalling interlude. She withdrew. She sat back. She let go of me with me dribbling with desire in front of her. Just for a moment, it would have been fun, a delicious torture and a renewed example of her mastery of me. But any serious delay would have unmanned me. I am able to get intellectual thrills from sexual activities and had done so earlier on in the night at some of the things we had got up to. But I was beyond that. I needed physical contact, fierce physical contact, and I needed it now. I wanted what was intimate, secret and forbidden. I knew her tongue was superb. Later I was to remember the various things she had done with it that evening and dwell on them, reliving the experiences over and over again. But for the moment I was in shock. My nerves had shattered. I didn't know what to do, but I had to do something.

My solution? An amazing act of selfishness, of courage. All I could do, the only thing that came to me, was to reach under me and grasp my cock and begin to work it. My cheek lay on the mattress, my face was screwed up as if in pain but I needed to see her, to see what she was doing.

She sat on her haunches staring at my arse, pretending not to notice I was frigging myself. Seething with terror and pleasure, I came almost at once to the point of climax. I could just see her breasts. They were out of my reach. They gave me pleasure, but I could do nothing for them. She leant forward a little. Almost stealthily she began to caress my thighs. She ran up the back of them, then she ran her fingers over my buttocks, and then between them. She was gentle, as if abstracted. Her fingertips trailed through my groin and touched the base of my belly. Then, with her open palms, she held my hips and pressed. She stared at me and I knew what was in her mind. I was on the rack. I began shouting again, just as I had shouted when she had taken her finger, wet from her mouth and from playing with the tip of my cock, to plunge into my anus.

Holding me between her hands, she lifted me slightly, raising my bottom further into the air, preparing it for what she intended. I relaxed my muscles as much as I could. Not that she needed my assistance, I was incapable of resisting her. I was the embodiment of docility. My muscles were jellied, my face was collapsing, her personality invaded mine. I felt her withdraw slightly. My arse grazed her stomach and we were too close for her to act.

She had been in this position with me, earlier, fulfilling my wildest dreams. Her body had driven me to a pitch of intense excitement then as she had presented it lewdly to me. But although women's bodies can do that to a man, men's bodies don't turn women on the same way. It wasn't worrying me. I simply waited for everything that was going to come my way. So maybe it wasn't my body, exactly, that aroused her so much. I think it was rather my own excitement, my own lusts, my own greed for her. And my obscenity, and my delight in hers, she loved that, too. That was how she was freed, that was how she was able to discover within herself and then reveal to me the impulses she had to do certain things. Even she was disconcerted by what welled up her. She freed me and made me over, but I freed her, too.

I had my eyes almost shut. But not quite – I could see her, see her face. It had changed again.

Since we had sat at table together in Antoine and Joelle's flat, she had been several different people. She had even had several different bodies, some clumsy, some dextrous. Thanks to her, I will never again judge women solely on their external appearance. After the first five minutes in my flat, it never made much difference anyway.

She was like someone in the room with you who is on the telephone. She was getting astounding news but she couldn't communicate it to the person in the room with her.

She lifted her hands, she held out her fingers. She might have been blind, trying to sense by touch what she should do next. Yet her eyes were open and she was watching all the time. For a fleeting moment I was in love. She struck me as inexhaustible, someone I could devote my whole life to.

She kept her lips closed but her breathing was powerful. Her breasts rose and fell. She looked at my cock which was up between my legs and pressed against my belly, like a torpedo ready for firing. She caught hold of it and bent it forwards herself. Her nails ran up and down its length whilst her fingertips caressed the shining knob as if to polish it. She released it as if a new thought had struck her, but I didn't worry. I knew she would be back. Her hands cupped my balls and fondled them. They hung softly but under her treatment they hardened, swelling up and lifting to become a single, hard, outraged sphere, sensitive to the slightest stimulation. It was obvious that she was leading up to something, paving the way and preparing me for a golden quarter of an hour. Now she lifted herself slightly and took her weight on her hands. She raised her groin and brought it towards me. She made a bridge between us, rubbing her wet oozing fanny against my glistening juicy arse. For the moment her hands were full. It wouldn't remain that way.

I said a quarter of an hour, but that was only a manner of speaking. What happened occupied a space of time, but since it changed me, it has never really stopped, so to speak. I remember a time hours, or maybe days, later, walking round my apartment, and realising that even my breathing had changed. Now I always breathe from the bottom of my chest. I'm not short of breath, or wheezing, or anything like that. Simply, I inflate my lungs differently, more fully, even in my sleep, I think.

Below my waistline I no longer exist. For a while, at least, I am drained of all tension. That, too, is new.

To go back to what we were doing. She began to push her fingers into me, first gently, then quickly, one after the other. The thumbs danced in me, she massaged me inside, she softened and loosened me, and then she filled me to the brim so that my arse was fat with her fingers. The woman in her knew that she must not stop, she must be everywhere at once, she must flood me, stuff me, overfill me. She violated my arse and she violated my soul. She knew no limits, save only that she took care not tear me with her nails.

She went down on me as if to hold me by force. She stiffened her index finger and her third finger and holding them together, she drove them into me and worked them like a piston. I found that being held down by her excited me more than anything. It made me feel raped.

She couldn't bear to get too hot, she couldn't bear to slow down. I adored her for it because it meant that every now and then she stopped, scooped her own juices from her foaming crotch, and used them to lubricate her frenetic invasion of my arse.

I was her empire, she had dominion over me. The more she saw how abased I was to her desires, the more she demanded my abasement. Yet she was eager that I should feel everything. She didn't want me afraid. She didn't hurt me with her fingers, her actions never descended into genuine brutality, so I was able to feel safe and to offer myself totally.

Though she held sway over me, she never went so far that physically or morally I lost stomach for it. She never turned me against her. The proof was in my cock – it seemed to double in size.

She entered me, she withdrew, she pushed back in, further in, with a slowness calculated to keep me just the right side of coming, on the edge but not over. Sometimes it was one great thrust with her bunched fingers. I could feel the urgency of her need, yet she controlled the speed.

It was too much for me, as an emotional experience. It was too new and all I could do was to brace myself to withstand the sexual and the psychological shocks. I was more exposed to her than she could have realised. I wanted only to thank her, over and over again. She permitted me to reveal my desires and longings more openly than even I had done within the safety of my own fantasies. That's why I don't really have the words to express myself properly. I hadn't even fantasised what we did, not all of it. I hadn't dared. She entered my dreams at the same time as she entered my reality at the same time as she entered my body with her probing fingers.

I hope I'm right in believing I will be a better person for that night, less pompous, more considerate. The same goes for my cock. Henceforward, it would be bigger, freer, cleverer. Over the years I had made attempts to improve the quality of my love-making, but they had been all too rare, tending to get lost in the moment of frenzy. No one before this had ever taken the time and the trouble with me that was needed. Liliane taught me so much that just the memory enables me to climax, to ejaculate, with no more stimulation than my cock brushing against my stomach.

I started to have convulsions, I think. My breathing exploded, I shouted madly, my voice went up and down. I was screeching, out of control. I long to have heard myself. She knew I was about to come. She left a thumb within me, still masturbating my anus. Her other hand she put into her vulva, slipping fingers into her cunt, in the place in women that I have yearned for since I was five years old.

We came together, crying: '*Fuck, fuck*!' Frantically she worked her thumb, keeping it within me as long as she dared. Then she got her hand under me, pulling my cock away from my belly and catching the spunk in the palm of her hand. Our hands were covered in it. They slid all around, in and out, I don't know how many fingers went where. I shook, I trembled violently – I was fulfilled.

She stopped. I had crossed the Rubicon. We might continue, we might not be done for the night, but the change had come about. The very rhythm and colour of life was different.

The flame of our lust had filled us. Now, gradually, it was dying back. Had it been a real fire, the embers still would have been glowing. Even when they turned black, a puff of breath would have brought them back to life. When eventually I opened my eyes, she was lying very close to me, her face against mine. She was trying to see me from as close as possible. She stroked my hair as if she really cared for me. I could not have borne it, had there been no light in the room then, for I would not have been able to read in her face the look of fascination it held.

8

It was Friday evening. We could have spent the weekend together, talking, sleeping together in the daytime, making pointless trips into the town and coming back to make love, at my place or at hers. But each of us had commitments on Saturday morning, and so we took leave of each other like robots. We might have been put together wrongly, or have parts missing, the way we moved. She had her car parked in the road, mine was in the underground car park.

She gave me a joy as unique as desire itself. Whether we meet again or not, she remains my first real friend.